Keisha & Trigga
A Gangster Love Story

LEO SULLIVAN

PORSCHA STERLING

D1521988

Text LEOSULLIVAN to 22828 to join our mailing list!

To submit a manuscript for our review, email us at
leosullivanpresents@gmail.com

© *2015*

Published by Leo Sullivan Presents

www.leolsullivan.com

Thanks From THE

AUTHORS!

First, I would like to thank God for allowing me to write with continuity. I have been in the game for over a decade and that is nothing but a testament to Him. I went from writing books in a penitentiary to luxurious penthouses in the sky.

I would also like to thank my family, the entire Sullivan Clan. Also, the fans that have supported me since the Triple Crown Publication days. I have to also thank my best friend, Taya R. Baker.

It was a pleasure to work with the very talented and extremely beautiful, Porscha Sterling. Thank you, love.

Don't forget to check out my new movie, Life Without Hope. It should be in theaters soon in 2016.

Also, to our real loyal fans please don't forget to leave a review. I read all of them. We promise not to keep you waiting on the next installment.

Sincerely,

Leo

I would like to thank all of my readers. I love you all. Many of you have been rocking with me since 3 Queens and I LOVE you for that.

Thank you to the many authors under Royalty Publishing House! You work hard so I work hard for you! Love you guys!

To the people who read my books for me in advance and inbox me their thoughts: Juanesia, Tanisha, Yolonda, Kitani….THANKS!!!!

Always gotta thank my baby for letting mommy be great. I love you, Alphonzo! You're my world and every breath I breathe is for you!

Leo, thanks for being you! I'm a hard author to work with but you know how to deal with me! <3

Porscha

ONE

Keisha snaked her leg around Lloyd's long, muscular body as she rubbed on his chiseled chest. The morning sun was teasing her eyelids as it pierced its rays through her silk curtains. Yawning, she nestled her head in the crook of Lloyd's neck and tried to enjoy a few minutes more being curled up next to her man as he slept peacefully.

Lloyd Evans was the epitome of what Keisha wanted in a man. Physically, he couldn't get no sexier. He stood at 6'4 and had the body of a basketball star with celebrity swag. There wasn't a bitch on Earth that he couldn't pull and she knew it, but he told Keisha every single day that he only had eyes for her. His dark chocolate skin was the reason for his street name, Black, and it didn't matter whom you spoke that name to, from the mayor to the crackhead, everyone knew who Black was. His Dominican maternal lineage gave him a faint accent, but he got his looks and cold demeanor from his father; a Jamaican goon who was as black as they came.

A blinking light caught Keisha's eye right before she was about to fall into a peaceful slumber and it jarred her fully awake.

His wife... Keisha thought to herself with disdain. She felt her body tense as the screen on his phone glowed continuously. Noting the shift in her embrace, Lloyd began stirring awake, which further annoyed her as she grew angrier with each second.

Dior Mitchell-Evans was the only black spot in Keisha's otherwise blemish-free relationship. When she first met Lloyd at *Pink Lips*, a strip club where she had been working as a bartender, he wasn't wearing a ring on his finger and didn't mention that he was married. After hearing Keisha drone on for weeks demanding to know why he always had to leave in the middle of the night and never stayed over, he finally told her the dirty truth. He was married to his high school sweetheart. Hurt by his revelation, Keisha threatened to break things off immediately, until he pulled out a stack of papers; divorce papers that he had been planning to have served to Dior as soon as he got a chance to get the financial details finalized.

Keisha swallowed her pride and reluctantly took him back, promising herself that she wasn't weak, but was actually doing her duty as a loyal woman who was willing to stay with her man until he got his shit together. Lloyd, happy as hell that she decided to stick it out with him, bought her a car, moved her into his condo, and gave her a monthly stipend, demanding that she never work at *Pink Lips* again.

It wasn't that she couldn't pull another baller because she could. With her smooth caramel complexion, light eyes and long straight hair that she kept cut in layers, she resembled a young Jada Pinkett-Smith, but she had the body of Nicki Minaj; thin in the waist, but fat in the ass. She could pull anybody walking in the club and she wasn't even on the stripper pole. But the fact was that she wanted Lloyd and, even though they had only been together about a year, she was caught up.

"Shit...what time is it?" Lloyd groaned as his eyes flickered open. Shifting in the bed, he nudged Keisha's leg from around him and sat up suddenly. "Fuck!" he yelled out, grabbing his phone from the nightstand next to him. "Why the hell didn't you wake me up?"

Frowning her face at his profile as he angrily scrolled through his phone, Keisha sat up next to him and pulled the covers up over her large, caramel breasts.

"What do you mean?" she huffed at him with a confused look on her face. She leaned over to the nightstand on her side of the bed and snorted up the rest of the lines that had been left from the night before. Wiping her nose in the crook of her arm, she waited for the high to overtake her as she watched Lloyd frown while continuing to go through his phone.

She didn't understand what the problem was. He never stayed over at her spot, so why did it matter that he did for one night? When Lloyd had fallen asleep after going at it for over four hours straight, she didn't bother to wake him. They snorted some coke together, then fucked the night away. After experiencing one of the best highs she'd had since he got her hooked a short time after they'd first met, she passed out right beside him. Him running home to Dior never crossed her mind and why should it? He was about to divorce her anyways, so Dior was already working with borrowed time .

"What I *mean* is that you know I don't fuckin' sleep over here." Lloyd stood up and started pulling on his clothes as Keisha watched him with her thick lips poked out in a small pout.

Lloyd ignored her as he gathered up the rest of his things and prepared to leave the luxury condo that he'd bought a few months back to stash her at. He didn't pay attention to her as she sat fuming at the foot of the bed watching him with her arms crossed because he knew she wasn't gonna do shit. Keisha was a good girl when he met her and he could see that right up front. But she was also a freak in disguise and he could tell that too. A little coke and a few drinks was all she had needed to turn right into the crazy, sexy chick he had needed her to be.

Keisha O'Neal was only 5'5 and her height wasn't the only thing that was a sharp contrast from the woman he had chosen to be his wife, who stood like a supermodel at 5'11. Like Dior, Keisha was a hood chick, but she was the quiet type who played her position and didn't give him any problems.

Dior, on the other hand, was the type to take off her $750 heels and pop a bitch in the mouth just on principle. She was a wild card, but she held Lloyd down when he was broke as hell and trying to come up. Back in the day, it wasn't nothing for her to slide a few baggies of coke up her pussy just to make sure that her nigga didn't catch a case. She was the definition of a down ass bitch, but she was also the definition of a crazy bitch, which was why he was trying to slide out of Keisha's spot as soon as possible. Dior knew too much about him for him to cross her and from the texts she'd sent, she was on the rampage.

"A'ight, I'm about to get up out of here," Lloyd told her as he looked at her from the living room. He flashed a sexy smile that showed off his bottom row of gold teeth and pulled his black hoodie around his shoulders. "What? You got attitude?" He flicked his tongue at her as he teased her. Keisha fought the smile that was teasing the sides of her lips.

"Hmph," she grunted, lifting her nose indignantly in the air. The subtle movement made the silk black sheets that she had draped around her body fall, showing off Lloyd's most favorite part of her body; her round pendulous breasts and perky nipples.

"Damn," he said grabbing his crotch through his black sweatpants. Keisha tried to fight it, but she couldn't help the way her eyes traveled to Lloyd's bulging anaconda dick that was standing up at attention. His sex drive was not affected at all by the rounds that he'd served up to her the night before.

"Bring that ass over here real quick," he commanded as he threw his backpack back down on the beige Berber carpet.

Twisting up her lips as she tried to save the little bit of attitude she had left, Keisha threw the sheets off the rest of her body and walked over to him. Lloyd slid his arms around her and scooped her up into a hug, squeezing her plump ass. Keisha snuggled in to him and was instantly caught up by the smell of his Versace cologne. She could already feel her high taking over as he held her. Her kitty thumped against his manhood and she wrapped her legs around his waist, opening herself up for him.

"Shit, ma, you know I gotta go—" Lloyd started, but was cut off suddenly when he heard the sound of someone banging on the front door. Tugging her legs from around him, Lloyd placed Keisha back on the floor.

"Who the fuck is that?" he asked her with a frown. Keisha shook her head, her lips partially parted with surprise while his dark brown eyes glared at her. "That bet not be no nigga coming to the shit I pay for!"

"I don't know who that is!" Keisha yelled out to him with pleading eyes. One thing she knew about Lloyd was that when he got angry, he went crazy. She'd heard a few things about what happened to those who crossed him and she vowed to never be one of the few.

Lloyd sneered at her before turning around to look for something as Keisha headed to the door. Lloyd reached for his chrome banger that he had stashed under the sofa, then happened to look up right as Keisha opened the door.

"Don't!" he shouted. But it was too late.

Keisha, reaching the peak of her high, made a crucial mistake in opening the door without looking through the peephole first. In the world of drug dealing, mayhem and murder, there was no room for such blunders. An unwanted intruder like the Feds, the Jack boys or an irate wife with a bad attitude looking forward to beating a side bitch's ass, could be the perilous consequence to such a mistake.

"TELL ME WHERE THE FUCK HE IS!" a chick with an angelic face and fiery red eyes yelled. She had the looks of a model and her ample breasts stood out like missiles as she glared down at Keisha, breathing hard, nostrils flaring. Noting that she was much taller than Keisha and assuming that she was stronger, she attempted to barge her way into the condo.

Keisha was completely taken by surprise at the bold chick's antics and moved in front of her in an attempt to block her path. They bumped like rams and shoved each other, then finally stopped and stood toe-to-toe.

"Bitch, you better get the fuck outta my way," the chick yelled in Keisha's face spraying her with spit. It was getting ready to pop off and fast!

"Bitch, who is YOU?!" Keisha yelled with a frown as she snaked her neck from side to side with clenched fists about to strike the chick in the face.

"I'm Dior Mitchell-EVANS, bitch! James Lloyd Evans' wife, that's who the fuck I am!"

Keisha's jaw dropped like she had rocks in her mouth. Dumbfounded, she looked at the tall buttery-complexioned woman with a pretty doll-baby face and slender long supermodel legs with a loss for words.

"Now get the fuck outta my way, bitch!" Dior screamed as she reached back to strike Keisha over the head with her oversized $3500 Ferragamo satchel.

Lloyd, who was watching the confrontation from behind Keisha, had been taken aback to see her as she waved her hand in Dior's face. Her current behavior was a sharp contrast from the woman he'd been in a relationship with over the past few months. She had seemed doe-like and unaggressive, but he was getting a quick lesson that she wasn't no punk.

Maybe it's the coke, he theorized. In a sick, twisted way, seeing her go head-to-head with Dior without a shred of fear slightly turned him on, but when he saw that things were about to get physical, he pulled himself back into reality.

Lloyd just happened to make it to the door and stepped between them in the nick of time as Dior swung the large bag and barely missed Keisha's face.

"Oh hell nah, BITCH!" Keisha yelled.

Instantly, like a deranged chick possessed with demons, Keisha completely lost it as she began to scream as she flailed her arms, kicking and swinging wildly while trying to get at Dior. It took everything in Lloyd's power to keep them apart. The two women began to exchange blows with Lloyd helplessly trapped in the middle getting pummeled with punches by both angry chicks as they went at it. Several of Keisha's kicks almost landed, hitting him in his testicles as he weaved and bobbed, struggling to keep the two women apart.

"Lloyd, I'ma beat this bitch's ass, then you next!" Dior shouted as she swung wildly.

"Really, BITCH? You gotta bring some ass to get some ass, hoe!" Keisha retorted as she jumped up and down on her toes swinging, steady throwing blows and trying to get a lick in. Somehow Lloyd had got his bottom lip busted and his ear stung from a slap across the head he had received by one of the females.

Finally, Lloyd separated them by shoving Keisha that so hard she stumbled and fell on her ass and was slow to get back up. Standing between the two women, he breathed heavily, panting for air and nearly exhausted. Too many blunts and not enough sleep combined with going at it all night with Keisha was starting to take its toll on him.

As Keisha rose to up from the floor, her robe had exposed her plump butt cheeks and a bold tattoo of Lloyd's name written in cursive red and blue across her ass. Thinking Lloyd was going to be hers forever, Keisha had hesitantly got the tattoo after Lloyd suggested she do something to prove her loyalty to him. Instantly, she'd regretted it, but there was no going back once it was done.

"Lloyd! I just know this fake booty, backwoods, gut bucket ass bitch ain't got yo-damn name tatted across her ass!" Dior yelled as her body went rigid. She was livid and tried to take a swing at him as her eyes welled with tears. He grabbed her hand, intercepting the blow.

"Come on, ma. Chill, man," he warned. He squeezed her hand, causing her to shrink in pain. He was letting her know that he meant business.

Dior pulled her hand away and thought about kicking him in his nuts, but she knew how violent he could be if she overstepped her boundaries. Instead, she mopped at her face with the back of her hand and fought a gall of emotion. She was determined not to cry.

Unlike Keisha, Dior knew the truth about Lloyd. Every other year she had to deal with him plucking up a tramp bitch from the sewers and laying her up in some random condo he would purchase downtown. He usually kept them for about a year or two until he got tired and moved on to the next one. Dior dealt with it as best as she could, telling herself that she was the one that he came home to each night, so it didn't mean nothing. But every single time Lloyd didn't bother to come home, she lost it.

"How many times we gotta go through this shit, nigga?!" Dior screamed at him. "How many times you gone leave my bed and use your dick to elevate the status of a busted, trash ass bitch?"

"Trash ass bitch?!" Keisha repeated and sucked her teeth in disdain as she pulled her robe closed. Looking down at her hand, she realized that two of her acrylic fingernails were broken all the way down to the core.

Lloyd scowled his discontent at his wife. This was the reason that he was honest with her...so that this type of shit wouldn't happen.

"Man, chill for real. I done told you about actin' like this," Lloyd warned her.

All of a sudden, Dior took a timid step back as she looked between the two of them and her tear-filled eyes turned into tiny slits of hate as she started to speak again.

"I swear… I'm so mothafuckin' sick of you…you lyin', cheatin' ass nigga!" Her bottom lip trembled like she was fighting the ebb and tide of her unbridled emotions. Still, she was determined not to cry as she clutched her round belly.

For the first time since Dior had showed up to the condo, Keisha's eyes dropped to her stomach and her heart broke with the realization of what she was seeing. Dior looked as if she couldn't be any less than five months pregnant.

Lloyd didn't respond. He just stood in the middle of them with a stoic expression and cast a wary glance down at the carpet. He hated when Dior panned him to the wall of his conscious every time she caught him like this. He never meant to hurt her, especially now with his seed growing in her belly.

Then suddenly like a dam erupting, Dior did what she was initially determined not to do. She broke down and cried poignantly, causing her body to rock with sobs. That tore Lloyd's heart apart as he watched a stream of tears pour down Dior's face. He resisted the urge to reach out and hold her golden cheeks with both hands.

"The hell?!" Keisha spat in contempt as she watched the display of emotion etched on Lloyd's face for his wife. Lloyd shot her a glare that would have scared a small child. It was his warning for her to fall back.

Dior turned to look at the hurt expression on Keisha's face, but she didn't feel a drop of sympathy. She was just one of the many women that she had caught Lloyd with over the years. There had been so many women that she'd long lost count and each time he got caught in the act he would lie and tell her that he was done and wouldn't hurt her again. The baby in her belly was supposed to be enough to make him stay, but it wasn't. She wasn't even six months along and here he was cheating again. She had fought dozens of women over her man. And if she stayed, she would fight dozens more.

Throwing her 10-carat canary diamond ring on the tile floor in the foyer, Dior decided that she was done.

"I want a divorce. I'm sick of dealing with your shit!" she told him.

"Cut that shit out, D," Lloyd said sucking his teeth. "We ain't gettin' no fuckin' divorce so dead that shit. And you already know I mean it."

At the mention of divorce, Keisha's ears perked up. With a confused expression on her face, she stepped forward.

"Um, what you mean you ain't gettin' no divorce? We already discussed it and you said you was getting rid of this bitch!" Keisha spoke to Lloyd, frowning at his back.

"Lloyd, you better tell your mutt to stay out of grown folks business, because I swear, I ain't gon' take too much more of this shit!" Dior warned him as she furtively looked for something to throw, or bust either of them upside the head with.

"Keisha, man, go to the fuckin' room," Lloyd told her with a sneer on his face. Keisha's eyes stretched wide with surprise when she looked in his eyes and noted that the care and love that he had in them when he looked at Dior was absent as he glared at her.

"I ain't doin' SHIT!" Kiesha spat as she tried desperately to save face although she knew that she was the loser in this situation. Angry and empowered by the drugs running through her, she stepped forward and mushed Lloyd in the head. "You can take your pregnant bitch and—"

WHAP!

Lloyd reached back and slapped her so hard and fast against the side of her face that it took a minute for the pain to register because of the state of shock she was in. Embarrassed and humiliated beyond belief, Keisha retreated, slightly staggering from the blow as she entered the master bedroom in tears. She'd never felt so ashamed in her entire young life. Pacing the large room, hatred quickly brewed in her heart as she occasionally wiped the blood spewing from her mouth with the back of her hand.

Keisha had been dealing with Lloyd for close to a year in hopes that he would one day replace Dior with her. But after today, she quickly realized that would never happen. As she choked back a pensive sob, she walked over to the bedroom door. She could vaguely hear Lloyd talking to his wife in a pleading voice that he had never used with her. With her, he was always 'Black' the boss who nobody questioned or dared to challenge. Now he was out there playing 'dearest husband' to Dior.

"Bae, I love you... I don't love that bitch. She just wanted to suck my dick and I know you have not been in the mood lately, so I let her do it once," Lloyd lied as Keisha eavesdropped.

"You lying again," Dior snapped. Keisha could hear them tussling.

"I swear to God on erra'thang I love." Lloyd struggled to hold Dior in his arms as she resisted.

"Then tell me why she got a tattoo of your name on her ass and she talkin' shit like she been your bitch for a while? And what's this about you sayin' we gettin' a divorce?"

"I dunno. She ain't shit to me. I love you."

"Then prove to me she ain't shit and call her out here and tell her to her face she ain't shit. I'm going to ask her if you fucked her and, nigga, if you lying..."

"I'm not lying."

"Call her out here then, nigga!!" Dior yelled.

"Keisha...come here!" Lloyd called out in his loud boisterous voice.

I know damn fuckin' well this nigga ain't about to try this shit, Keisha seethed. *He must really think I'm a dumb bitch, but I got his ass.*

High as hell and hurt more than she'd ever been in her entire life, Keisha staggered slightly after standing up from the bed. Rummaging through the top drawer of her large mahogany dresser,

Keisha tossed her lace panties to the side and grabbed the small Glock pistol that she made sure to always keep handy to protect herself. She walked out the bedroom startling both of them as she stood in the hallway of her luxury condo and aimed with a trembling hand with tears streaking down her face as she cocked the gun and aimed.

CLICK!

Both Dior and Lloyd turned to see Keisha holding the gun aiming back and forth between both their heads.

Aghast, Lloyd could barely contain the terror in his voice when he spoke to Keisha in a timorous tone as he took several steps towards her.

"Keesh, wha...what you doin'?! Put dat shit down, you trippin' man."

"Naw'll you trippin' nigga if you think I'ma just lay down and let you play me like a fuckin' joke!" Keisha said as she cried harder; her voice of reasoning shrinking with each tear. She aimed the gun at Dior's stomach.

"Lloyd!" Dior cried out, alarmed for the safety of her unborn child.

As only Lloyd knew all too well, too much coke and not enough sleep was a recipe for disaster for any junkie, but for Keisha, it was much worse because she was heartbroken and distraught on top of it all.

Daringly, Lloyd took another step towards Keisha and the loaded gun.

"Shawty, give me the burner—"

Too late.

BLOCKA! BLOCKA! BLOCKA!

A barrage of shots rang out.

TWO

Lloyd reached for the gun just as Keisha began firing. He felt torrid heat pierce his right arm as he wrestled the gun away from her and slapped her across the face. She collapsed in a heap, sliding down the wall and began to hysterically cry to herself.

What the hell is happening to me? she wondered. Lloyd had her all messed up in the head, competing for the love of a nigga who didn't give a fuck about her.

Dior just stood there with her face ashen pale. She was in a trance-like state of shock, as she thought about how she had come within seconds of losing her life. One thing was for certain, call it her womanly instinct, or whatever you chose, but she was certain the bitch, Keisha, was crazy as fuck and there was now no doubt in her mind that Lloyd and the chick were in a serious relationship and he was fucking her good.

Lloyd turned to her grim-faced. One of the bullets had grazed his right arm. He was leaking blood from the superficial wound. He held the gun he'd taken from Keisha as she wailed pitifully, lying against the wall.

"Bae, just go wait for me out front, lemme handle this." Lloyd tried to placate his wife with a soft voice and a gentle hug. The whole while Keisha cried. Dior shoved him away like he was contaminated with the Ebola virus and screamed to the top of her lungs at him.

"Fuck you. I'm tired of your no good cheating ass!" Dior lashed out. "I know you're fucking this hoe, because ain't no bitch going to be all in her feelings like this," Dior fumed then added on a second note. "I'm sick and tired of you. When you get home, I want you to get your shit and get out."

As Dior made her exit, Lloyd shook his head and turned to Keisha. He understood that Dior was mad, but he knew he could get her back. She wasn't going anywhere.

Keisha was another problem; he had too much stock invested in her cocaine-snorting ass. The bitch had damn near killed him and his wife. But he had to admit Keisha had some good ass pussy and some smoking head. Plus, when she was high, she would even do all the freaky shit his wife wouldn't do like the backwards cowgirl and let him hit her in the ass. A nigga be loving that wild shit, but the real center of his desire was that he kept his work at the spot he got her. He could count on her not to touch it, or his money. He wasn't going to keep it where he laid his head at night and Dior wasn't having that anyways.

He looked down at a hole in his $2,000 Versace shirt and then at Keisha as she boo-hoo cried. She was looking pathetic with her mascara running and her short hair in disarray all over her forehead.

"I should beat your ass for this shit, but I won't. No more coke for you."

Keisha started crying even harder and Lloyd couldn't tell if it was because of him, or because he threatened her with no more coke. As soon as he found another spot to stash his product and a bitch thorough enough to watch it without messing with it and swallow up his dick good as she did, he was kicking her out on her ass. The ride had been good and sometimes he did get caught up when he was around her. But he wasn't crazy. He couldn't fall in love no matter how bad she was.

"Get in the bed and go to sleep," he demanded and then looked at his arm.

He needed to get to a hospital, a clinic or something. The blood continued to roll down his arm and the droplets hit the floor. Even though the bullet only grazed him with a flesh wound, it still hurt like hell.

Grabbing his backpack off the floor, he walked out the door and locked it behind him, leaving Keisha still sobbing in the bed.

***

Kenyon watched from the window of his dark blue Aston Martin as Dior walked out of the front entrance of Lloyd's condo that he shared with his side bitch, Keisha. He'd only seen Keisha one time since Lloyd kept her tucked away hidden at his downtown condo. He became aware of Lloyd's new plaything when he had been told to meet him there to pick up some work. She was nice looking and had a banging ass body complete with curves in all the right places, but she also had an innocence about her that let Kenyon know she wasn't cut out for Lloyd no matter how hard she tried to act on the outside.

On his way over to meet Lloyd at his crib that morning, he was about to make a right into the golden-gated entrance when he saw Dior tearing out of the estate in her all-white Bentley. Immediately, he knew something was wrong and he knew it had to do with Lloyd's inability to keep his dick in his pants.

Gritting his teeth, Kenyon decided to follow Dior; although he knew in his mind that it was the wrong thing to do. Lloyd never let too many men around Dior because she was his prize; the one woman ever street nigga wanted, a chick who was willing to do whatever for the man she loved. Coupled with her loyalty was a pretty face and a bad ass body. She looked like she was made to walk down the Victoria's Secret runway with her long, slender, golden-colored legs.

The only reason Kenyon had been able to get close to her was because he was Lloyd's cousin and also one of his most trusted men in his crew. Kenyon's and Lloyd's fathers hustled side by side in Jamaica before they were killed in a deal gone wrong. Carrying on with their legacy, Kenyon and Lloyd did things the same way as their fathers, but they grew up more like brothers than cousins, so their bond had been stronger.

It was that bond that made Kenyon feel guilty for how he felt about Dior. Over the nine years that she had been married to Lloyd, Kenyon had watched him use her over and over again to help push his dope all around the States when he was coming up. After he established his place as a boss hustler he married her, but instead of treating her like the treasure she was, he rewarded her sacrifice and loyalty by cheating on her with any and every bitch that looked like she had good pussy.

From what he'd seen of Keisha, she wasn't his normal type. She looked like a good girl, but he knew that shit wouldn't last. Lloyd had a way of turning the best women sour. He was toxic.

Under Kenyon's watchful gaze, he watched as Dior used a car key and drug it all through the candy red paint of Lloyd's Maserati that was parked out front. Then she pulled out a metal object from her purse and flattened all four tires. After what seemed like a couple minutes of deep thought, she turned to the white Bentley that she had driven there in and drove the metal through all four of those tires as well.

Kenyon shook his head and chuckled lightly as he looked at her. One thing about Dior was that she didn't just lay down and take no shit. Yeah, she would probably be taking Lloyd back later, but she always made sure to make that nigga pay.

As Dior took off in a mad strut down the road and away from the condo, Kenyon started in a slow creep behind her. It didn't take long for him to see from the expression on her face, that she had no idea where she was going, or how she was going to get there. Slowly, he crept up beside her and rolled down the window.

"What's good, ma? That belly got you looking mad sexy. Can a nigga get them digits?"

Turning towards him, a look of surprise ignited in her almond-shaped brown eyes when she saw who was speaking to her. Even though she was still seething from dealing with Lloyd, she couldn't help but half-smile at Kenyon's playful attitude. He always knew how to deal with her when she got upset.

"Ken, what you doing here?" Dior asked rubbing her hand over her belly. She hadn't walked far, but she was dead tired from strutting around with a bulging belly in 5-inch stilettos.

"Looking at you," Kenyon teased making Dior's half smile into a full grin through her smudged mascara and puffy red eyes. "Listen yo, I'm gon' hit you wit' some game. You supposed to fuck *that* nigga shit up—not yo' own shit. Ain't that like woman code or sumthin'?" He gestured towards her damaged Bentley.

"Yeah," she said with a slightly embarrassed look on her face. "So….can I get a ride?"

"Hell, naw. I'mma make yo' pregnant ass walk for that shit. Never in life are you supposed to do that kinda shit to a Bentley as fly as the one you got. I should perform a citizen's arrest on yo' ass for that shit!" Kenyon joked. Dior kicked her hip out to one side and placed her hand on it while rolling her eyes at him.

"Let me get your door," he said with a light chuckle.

Kenyon jumped out from his side of the car and jogged over to the passenger side to open the door for her.

"Thank you," Dior said breathlessly.

Without a word, Kenyon ran back around and sat back down in his seat, then drove off. He was about to continue on down the road when he turned suddenly to look at Dior. Although her head was turned away from him, he could tell that she was crying. Swerving to the right, he pulled his car into the front of a Quick Trip gas station they were about to drive by. He put the car in park and sighed, internally fighting himself for what he was about to say.

"Listen, D," he started. Dior turned to look at him as she wiped her face with the back of her hand. "I know I joke around a lot but this is some serious stuff right here I'm about to say. I know Lloyd got you going through some shit. He always got you going through some shit. But anyways…I want you to know that I'm here and I got you no matter what."

Sniffing, Dior leaned over and placed her hand on top of his. Kenyon automatically responded by flipping his hand around to hold hers. Dior immediately felt a warm feeling move throughout her body and it soothed her as she looked into Kenyon's light brown eyes.

At 6'3, Kenyon was a tad bit shorter than his older cousin, but was just as respected. Like Lloyd, Kenyon was ruthless and had a reputation that let everyone know he wasn't the type of nigga you fucked with. But that was where their similarities ended. Kenyon had a cool demeanor and was the quiet one out of the two. Lloyd was more of a people's person when the time was right, but Kenyon always hung back in the shadows and let him shine. With his light toffee-colored complexion, long lashes and effortless swag, many mistook him for a ladies' man, but that wasn't him at all. He wasn't checking for women even though they were always checking for him. And the fact that he stayed in the gym didn't help much.

"I'm serious," he repeated to her. "If you ever need me, all you gotta do is call and I'm coming."

It was then that it dawned on him that they were still holding hands. Dior squeezed his gently and looked into his eyes, saying in a somber tone, "Thank you, Ken." She released his hand and turned to look out of the window letting off a deep sigh. "I need someone in my corner for what I'm about to do."

"What's that?" he asked her with a frown.

"I don't know yet, but I want Lloyd to pay for everything he's done to me. It won't be bad, but I just can't let him get away with everything…" Suddenly, Dior turned and looked at him, a light shining behind her eyes. "Wait…will you help me if I need it?"

A crease formed in Kenyon's forehead as he listened to what she was saying. It was bad enough that he was having feelings for his cousin's wife, but now she was asking him to help her get revenge on him for all the messy shit he'd put her through. He wanted no parts. He couldn't get caught up in Lloyd's bullshit.

"If you help me with Lloyd, I'll do anything… I mean anything." She then leaned forwarded and kissed him softly on the cheek, as she grabbed his hand again.

Right as Kenyon was about to say something, her cellphone chimed. Dior looked at her purse and hesitated, afraid that it was Lloyd. The last thing she wanted was another confrontation with him.

Kenyon squeezed her hand before gesturing with his chin and head held high when he said with a confidence he had never felt before.

"Answer it."

"Where you at?" Lloyd's voice boomed through her ears.

Clicking her tongue, Dior spat into the phone with attitude, "That's none of your business anymore, Lloyd. We're through."

"Is that so?" Lloyd asked coldly. His tone threw her off because he'd never used that particular one with her, but she recovered quickly.

"Yes, it is. Like I said, I want you to have your stuff out as soon as possible. Unless you plan to fight me for the house?" she asked him knowing very well that he would never try to battle her for anything in court.

"I done already told your ass to kill that divorce shit. It ain't happenin'. We'll talk about this at the house when I get there," Lloyd told her.

"Ain't nothin' changing, but that's fine. I'll see you then."

Dior hung up the phone without another word. She then turned to Kenyon who had been watching her intensely. After a second of looking at each other, it seemed that both of them were thinking the same thing. They were playing with fire and the idea that they were toying with could never be.

Pulling out from in front of the gas station, Kenyon gunned his whip off down the road in a hurry. At the time, neither of them saw Lloyd standing in the cut watching them suspiciously.

THREE

Keisha was in a half-daze. She was high as hell and so numb that she couldn't even feel her toes. Matter of fact, she couldn't feel any of her limbs. But the one thing she could feel was the only thing that she had wanted to numb; her aching heart.

Four days after the incident with Lloyd and Dior, Lloyd had cut his losses and tossed her out on her ass. He gave her a wad of money, had someone pack a few of the clothes that he'd bought her into a suitcase, and then sent her on her way. Keisha still wondered to herself who it had been that had packed her clothes so neatly. There was no way that it was Lloyd.

It probably was the next bitch he movin' in there, Keisha thought to herself as she peeked out through her eyelids. She slowly brought her hand up to her mouth and wiped away the pool of slob from the side of her face. The entire part of the pillow under her was drenching wet with her saliva.

Keisha was lying in The W hotel room that she had reserved for herself after Lloyd kicked her out. As soon as she threw her stuff in the room and got over her anger at being tossed out by someone she thought loved her, she realized that she needed help coping with her hurt and anger. So she grabbed her purse and went to East Point where she knew she could buy some dope from one of Lloyd's corner boys and made her way back to the hotel to enjoy her high.

Now all of the baggies that she'd had were gone after only three days. She'd been snorting constantly for most of the day to keep her high, but at this point it seemed like she wasn't able to reach the height that she'd wanted. So she grabbed the last baggie he'd sent her that contained a crack rock, something she'd never tried before. In hopes of reaching the high she craved, she went to the corner store to grab what she needed and smoked it all away.

But now she felt like shit.

That muthafucka sold me the cheap shit!

Keisha rolled over on the bed and looked up at the ceiling. It was dark out and she had no idea what time it was, but what she did know was that she wasn't far from Lloyd's condo. Maybe if she went back over there he'd let her give him some head for some of the good shit. He'd always liked her mouth work and it was her last hope, because the stack that he'd given her was nearly gone.

Ten minutes later, Keisha was standing outside of the building that housed the condo that she had shared with Lloyd and her head was spinning. Instead of the euphoric feeling that she was used to, she was dizzy and to top it off, she could feel a headache approaching. The thought of it all made her mad as hell. She was so used to Lloyd's premium dope that her body wasn't responding right off the watered down shit that niggas were serving in the hood.

"It's okay," Keisha said out loud to herself. She would be able to get the good stuff soon.

But first she had to figure out a way to keep her head from spinning, so she could figure out which of the five buildings she saw swirling in front of her was the one Lloyd lived in. Her vision was blurred and she was seeing objects in triple.

Keisha leaned on a car near her and felt herself getting dizzier by the second. Her hearing was magnified to the point that it seemed like every sound was blaring right in her ears. She covered her face with her hands and tried to get herself together, but she could feel herself begin to panic.

She was hallucinating.

She heard voices around her; people were laughing and rap music was blasting in her ears. But she couldn't see anything because the images before her were swirling in front of her eyes. Keisha felt her knees grow wobbly as she began to breathe in quick, sharp breaths.

Am I dying? she thought to herself. She grabbed at her chest and felt as if she could feel her rapidly beating heart through the thin, sheer red blouse that was draped over her trembling shoulders.

Falling to her knees in a panic as the voices around her grew louder, she tried to duck under the large SUV she had been leaning on, thinking that she had found a nice place to hide from the voices. But they continued. Laying sideways under the SUV, Keisha tucked her knees to her chest and hugged her body tightly as she lay on the ground and started to cry. She prayed to God that the voices would soon stop.

Off in the cut, someone had been watching Keisha the entire time and she didn't even know it. Trigga shook his head as he looked at the junkie in front of him. How people were able to get hooked on shit that had them looking like a muthafuckin' fool half the time was beyond him. Trigga didn't drink or smoke and had never done a drug a day in his life—besides the occasional blunt here, or there. But weed was natural so, to him, it didn't count. His twin brother, Mase, said it was because he was a control freak and didn't like the feeling of something invading his body and making him unable to control every single one of his actions. However, Trigga used the shit-faced girl across the street from him as more evidence as to why he stayed away from the stuff.

He continued to watch her intently, although he didn't quite know why. The whole scene was just sad. She looked like she could have been attractive had it not been for her current state. She was high as hell, her hair was strewn all over her head and her clothes were wrinkled and didn't match. She was wearing one flip-flop and one flat closed-toe ballerina shoe.

As he watched, he saw that she seemed to be spazzing more and more with each moment. She was covering her ears with her hands and her eyes were open wide as if she was terrified. Trigga narrowed his eyes and peered at her while turning his loud rap music down. A group of white teens, two guys and one chick, walked pass her and started laughing loudly as they looked at her.

"Look, it's a crackhead!" the girl yelled out and they all started laughing and pointing at the woman. Their voices seemed to scare her to death. She searched around with her eyes looking aimlessly around her as if she didn't know where the noise was coming from.

Shaking his head once more, Trigga frowned and sighed. There was something about three white kids pointing and laughing at a black woman that didn't sit right with him. He had some other shit that he'd wanted to tend to, but this suddenly became priority…at least for the moment.

Pulling the door open to his silver Audi R8, Trigga jumped out and started walking towards the woman with a clenched jaw. He was mentally fighting against his urge to help her the entire way. It wasn't in his nature to step into a situation that wasn't his, but call it chivalry or whatever you like, he couldn't let this woman stay here in her current state without helping. For some reason, she reminded him of his mother. And he'd done everything in his power to protect his mother.

"Aye, shawty…" Trigga said once he reached the woman.

She had climbed underneath the black Cadillac that she'd been leaning on and from her labored breathing that he could hear from where he stood, she was still scared to death.

Trigga leaned down to look at her and noticed that she was moving back and forth as she lay on the ground, sweating profusely and scratching at her neck. Her long hair was plastered to her head, held down by the sweat that was dripping down her face. From the way that her eyelids were opening and closing, he could tell she was going in and out of consciousness. He'd seen this before plenty of times. She got hold of some bad dope and she was trippin'. Nothing left to do, but to sleep off the high.

Trigga reached under and grabbed at the woman's shoulder.

"Aye, I'mma help you, a'ight?" he said.

Panicked, Keisha started kicking as hard as she could at the stranger that she felt grab her by the arm. She didn't know who he was or what he wanted, but she had an idea. She was alone at night and she was high. He was going to rape her and she couldn't let him violate her in that way. Keisha used all the strength she had, which wasn't a lot to begin with, and started fighting and lashing out with all her might at her assailant.

"Get the fuck away from me!" she yelled out as he grabbed at her ankles. Every time she felt his hand on her, she would kick it away.

"Stop…shit! Gotdammit, I'm tryin' to help yo' ass! Who the fuck you related to—Jackie Chan or some shit?" the man yelled out, but Keisha wasn't backing down.

Well, not until a wave of exhaustion hit her like a brick and she felt her strength leave her body.

Her kicks came slower and became softer as she started to feel her eyes close unwillingly. Her mind was racing, but her body was moving in slow motion. Then suddenly her entire body went limp and she fell back, flat onto the concrete. She felt a hand on her leg and, though she tried to fight back, she failed miserably as the man pulled her out from under the car.

The next morning, Keisha woke up back in her suite at The W hotel. The sheets beneath her were drenched with sweat, she had a splitting headache and her mouth was dry as sandpaper. As she sat up, she squinted at the sunlight that entered the room and assaulted her sensitive eyes.

Looking down at her soiled, mismatched and wrinkled clothes, the memory from the night before interrupted her consciousness and she began frantically probing her body with her hands to assess any damage the man had caused. But there was none.

Was I dreaming? Keisha thought as she rubbed the back of her head.

She knew she hadn't been dreaming about the bad dope because she could still feel the after effects of it. But had she been dreaming about the man who had been trying to rape her?

Pulling off the tiny shorts she was wearing, she examined her lace purple panties. Nothing seemed to be out of place. Then she opened them and peered inside. Still nothing seemed wrong. Rubbing her thighs together, she tried to see if she could feel any soreness in her most sacred spot that would point towards assault. There was nothing.

"Maybe it was a dream," she mumbled to herself with a croaky voice that resembled a grumpy, ninety year old man.

Just as she was about to stand up from the bed, she noticed something on the nightstand that made her pause. A letter written on the hotel's stationary. She grabbed it and read it with a frown.

Dear Ms. Jackie Chan, You lucky that it was me who saw you and not some grimy nigga. Stay the fuck off that shit.

With wide eyes, Keisha held the letter in her hands and thought about its words. So the man *was* real, but he hadn't tried to rape her at all. He'd saved her.

Stay the fuck off that shit, he'd said. Something about that statement resonated with her as she thought about the events of the night before and how terrified she'd been.

Tears came to her eyes as she thought about how much danger she could have been in the night before if he…whoever he was…hadn't been the one to find her. Keisha folded the paper into a small square and tucked it in her bra, close to her heart. She closed her eyes and made a promise to herself and to God that she would try to be sober. She never wanted to experience a night like last night ever again.

Looking on the nightstand, she saw something else. A prepaid Visa gift card and another note.

I would leave you cash, but I'm guessin that wouldn't be smart on my behalf, huh? Get yo' ass out of bed, buy some clothes that cover your WHOLE ass, get something to eat and get yourself together.

Keisha smiled to herself as she looked at the second note and laughed at the joke about giving her cash and covering her whole ass. Then she folded that note up as well and stuck it into her purse. Gripping the gift card in her hand, she stood up and walked to the shower to get cleaned up. She didn't know if she would be able to shake her habit, but she wanted to start.

For the first time since he'd kicked her out four days ago, Keisha thought of someone other than Lloyd and wondered if she'd ever meet the man who had saved her life again.

FOUR

Three Weeks Later

"Look, I told your ass to leave out of here, Keisha," Cash barked at her as she stood in front of his large wooden desk with her hands on her hips. He sat back in his seat, crossing his arms in front of his large, flabby chest as she tried to bat her eyes at him. The greasy, dark-skinned, rotund man blinked blankly at her and shook his head.

"Your looks ain't gone do shit for me unless you about to use them pretty green looking eyes of yours and fat ass to twirl around on that pole out there and make me some of my damn money back. Now, I want you out of here!"

Keisha groaned, rolled her eyes to the ceiling and tugged at her now short hair. Wanting a change of hair to go with her new life, she'd gone to the salon and got her hair cut into a short pixie cut. It was cute and she worked it well, but it still didn't score any points with Cash. She knew Cash was going to give her a hard time but she didn't think it would be this damn hard. But true to his name, Cash was only about that green and since Keisha had been responsible for him missing out on a few dollars a while back, he was unforgiving.

"But Cash, you *know* I wouldn't come here asking you for shit if I didn't need it. You *know* that! I really need my old job back. I don't have anything else and I need the money."

"And I *needed* the money when you decided to waltz your ass out of here without giving me nothing, but a couple minutes' notice because you found yourself a paid nigga who ain't want you workin'. Now what done happened? He had his fill and told your ass to kick rocks?"

Cash leaned back in his seat and smirked at her, showing off the four solid gold teeth that his first big check from *Pink Lips* paid for. Sliding a thin toothpick through the middle of a gap in his teeth on the side of his mouth, he rubbed his round belly and waited for her answer.

Keisha sighed and slid her fingers through her short hair, not wanting to get into what had happened almost four weeks ago at the condo with Lloyd and Dior.

"Cash, just know I need this and I will do whatever you want to repay you."

"Whatever I want, hm?" Cash asked with a twinkling in his eye that made Keisha grimace. She let her silence be her answer as she waited for his demands.

"Ok!" Cash clapped his pudgy hands together as a wide smile spread across his face. "You work the first week with no pay and I'll think about letting you back in here for good."

Keisha's face lit up and she had to stop herself from running over to grab Cash and pull him into a hug.

"Thank you so much! I promise that I won't leave you hanging like that again, I swear!" Keisha promised. She grabbed her Chanel bag off the small table next to the door and turned around to leave. Before she could, Cash stopped her.

"Listen, Keesh, take all that rich shit you got on off," he said referring to the royal blue Prada dress and Balenciaga heels that Lloyd had bought her. "Put something on that shows off that ass and those round tits. The girls in the back should be able to lend you something. One of my other bartenders quit last week so I need you to start tonight."

Keisha grew tense immediately and Cash could see it even with her back to him. Truth was, she had the job as soon as she walked in asking for it. He needed a replacement for the last chick who had quit and he hadn't been able to find one with the banging ass body that he knew his patrons enjoyed to watch as they waited for their drinks. But he knew Keisha was desperate when she walked in so he decided to get some payback.

Whipping around, Keisha opened her mouth to speak, "So you *needed* me—"

"Let's just call it even!" Cash told her with a sly grin, holding his hands in the air as if to surrender.

Furious, Keisha turned around and stormed out the door.

That muthafucker… she thought.

***

"Girl, you gotta get some life in ya if you want these tips," Tish said as she poured up a Crown and coke for an older gentleman who was having a more entertaining time watching her bountiful bosom sway from side to side as she made his drinks than the show the stripper on the pole was giving.

With pursed lips, Keisha looked at Tish and nodded her head. She knew that Tish was right. Keisha had only been working for about two hours so far and practically had to beg to take someone's drink order. Tish, on the other hand, was racking them in.

To top it off, Tish wasn't even no dime piece. She wasn't ugly and she had a nice body, but she had a jagged scar that extended from above her right eye and went all the way down to her chin. Tish did a good job of trying to cover it with her thick, long black hair, which she draped to one side, Aaliyah-style.

Whoever the man belonged to that Tish must have been fuckin' around with gave her ass the business once she found out, Keisha thought to herself.

Looking at it made her think of Lloyd. Oh, how she wished she had been able to pop a cap in his cheating ass.

"Here," Tish said, slamming a shot glass on the table. "Take this one," she slammed another shot glass down beside it. "And this one. It's a special concoction I made and it's sure to loosen you up a bit."

Grabbing the glass between her pink manicured fingers, Keisha frowned her eyes up at Tish before taking a whiff of the mixture. It was so strong one sniff nearly burned her nose hairs.

"What is *this*?" Keisha asked wrinkling up her nose as she peered at the brown liquid.

She had been off coke since the day that she'd woke up in the hotel with the note from the mystery man who had saved her. Although she had wanted to quit after the incident with Dior and Lloyd, he'd kicked her out of four days later and she needed help dealing with the stress. With a wad of cash and a suitcase full of the clothes that he'd bought her, Lloyd had sent her on to find her own way.

"Try it. I promise it will help." Tish winked at her then turned away to tend to another patron.

Keisha swallowed down both glasses of liquid quickly, wincing from the burn as it traveled through her body.

Pulling at a loose strand of hair that was tickling her ear, Keisha let her eyes roam the area. The smoke was thick in the dimly lit club. Streaks of fluorescent strobe lights pierced the air as strippers of all shapes and sizes walked about ready and willing to provide whatever services were required of them. Cash always told the patrons with the fattest wallets that his club didn't condone sex for pay, but his statement was always concluded with a wink to let everyone know what was really up.

Coming back to work at *Pink Lips* was the last thing that Keisha had wanted to do, but after cleaning herself up, she sat down with a guidance counselor at Clark Atlanta University to tell her what she needed to do in order to get in that Fall. Based on Keisha's stellar high school career, she was a shoe-in and could start the next semester…as long as she was able to cover 60% of the tuition. She used the last of the money that she got from Lloyd to make a down-payment on the total cost of her contribution and paid rent at the small one bedroom apartment she was living in, then sucked in her pride and drove down to *Pink Lips* to ask for her job back. It wasn't the best situation, but it could be worse, so she vowed to make it work.

***

Across from where Keisha stood, staring off into space and waiting until it was time to clock out, Trigga was sitting glowering at his twin brother, Mase. Mase was having the time of his life, popping champagne on the wide backside of an ebony-colored stripper like he was unconcerned about the serious fact that they were in Atlanta to murder one of the most ruthless cold-blooded dudes in the city. And just by what was going on in the club, it wasn't going to be an easy task by any stretch of the imagination to murder Lloyd.

Although Trigga was only twenty-seven years old, he didn't gain enjoyment from spreading dollars on the oily manufactured bodies of women who would do anything to be rewarded by his cash. He enjoyed handling his business and had a reputation for doing so.

He had rightfully earned the nickname Trigga for a reason. He wasn't afraid to pull the trigger and had killed for the first time when he was thirteen; his stepfather, right in front of his mother and twin brother. His stepfather had been beating the shit out of his mother and even at a young age, Trigga didn't hesitate to do what he had to do.

"You want a dance *papi*?" a Puerto Rican cutie by the name of Luxe asked Trigga as she walked up to him.

Luxe was one of the top paid strippers at the establishment and it was easy to see why. What she didn't have in breasts, she made up for in ass and she had thighs so thick that it was a marvel that she could support them with her itty, bitty waist. Her long, curly blond hair hung all the way down to the top of her globe-like booty cheeks and she always sported 7-inch stiletto heels to make sure that her backside rotated as she walked.

Noting the quiet gentleman in the corner of his establishment who looked like he would be a definite big spender, Cash sent Luxe over to tempt Trigga into parting with some of his dollars. But Trigga wasn't interested or impressed.

"Nah, I'm good," he said looking up.

It was then that he happened to notice the bartender at the horseshoe-shaped bar tending to patrons as the club's strobe lights ricocheted, bouncing off the elegant crystal glass and exotic mirrors. Smoke billowed like a halo around her pretty face and he found himself staring as if hypnotized. There was something about the female bartender that held his attention. She was beautiful, with her hair in a short, classy style. He could see the curvy outline of her figure then she smiled, displaying perfect ivory colored teeth.

"What da fuck," he muttered to himself, snapping out of the momentary trance and tore his eyes way from her.

M.O.B was his motto: Money Over Bitches. So instead, he shifted his eyes towards the nigga named Lloyd, or Black, as Queen, the woman who had contracted him, said he was also known as. He was the leader of a treacherous crew known as *E.P.G.* which stood for East Point Gangstas. East Point was one of the most dangerous places in Atlanta known for murder, drugs and extortion and Black was the ringleader.

One thing for certain, whatever the fuck the nigga name is, him and his E.P.G. goons are going to be a problem, Trigga thought as he watched them turning up bottles and making it rain.

Trigga felt a pang of hatred as he watched Kenyon, who he was told was Lloyd's cousin, reach into a large black garbage bag and pull out a wad of cash so big that when he slung it, he hit a stripper in the face making her stumble over and fall on her ass. The club's patrons and all of Lloyd's goons got a good laugh out of it. Everybody except Trigga. He made a mental note to place a bullet between Kenyon's eyes too.

The entire crew of rowdy thugs had just about every stripper in the club at their tables competing for a lap dance as they popped bottles and smoked loud without a care in the world while they continued tossing big face hundred dollar bills

With the help of Queen, Trigga had done his homework and had quickly learned that Lloyd was a major player in Atlanta's lucrative drug trade and also that Lloyd was part of an elaborate crew that kidnapped and robbed rival drug dealers.

Trigga and his brother had been hired specifically by Queen to come all the way from New York City to murder him. Lloyd was responsible for killing her brother, Jawell, and stealing about a hundred grand in coke and money. Queen didn't give a shit about the money and drugs, but she wouldn't stop until she knew Lloyd was dead for killing Jawell.

Queen vowed that there would be hell to pay. She placed a one million dollar bounty out on Lloyd and two million if he was brought to her alive. She even placed a bounty on any member of his family, including Lloyd's mother, dead or alive, and advised Trigga and his brother to kill everyone who Lloyd loved. Trigga wasn't game for killing innocent people, but he had no problem murking Lloyd, or his grimy cousin, Kenyon.

Trigga thought that he and his brother, Mase, would have a tough time finding Lloyd since word was that he knew Queen was looking for him. But Lloyd and his goons were incredibly bold, and with good reason. From what Trigga could see, they all were in the club strapped with bangers the size of army guns and had a notorious reputation for homicide. It was obvious to Trigga that murking Lloyd was going to be difficult, if not impossible.

Another troubling issue was his twin brother, Mase. For some reason he was acting strange, as if murdering Lloyd while he stood with half a dozen goons wasn't going to be a problem. The only concern Mase had was spending money, poppin' bottles and stuntin' like he had more money than he did to impress the bitches.

They hadn't even been in the club an hour and Mase had already hit Trigga up for some more bills.

Lloyd got up and tossed what looked like a bale of money at the strippers and watched with delight as a melee broke out between a stripper and some chick with a bangin' body and bluish hair. The two chicks went at it blow-for-blow swinging wildly as three burly bouncers rushed over to break up the fight.

Lloyd seemed to be oblivious to the fight as he wavered, teetering on his feet with a bottle of Patron in his hand, and staggered across the club. Trigga followed him with his eyes, the whole while his heart was beating faster. He hoped that Lloyd was headed for the restroom. If so, that was where he intended to kill him. He looked over at his brother to get his attention, but Mase was into a lap dance that he was receiving from a redbone with her hair shaved on the sides and a flaming red Mohawk at the top.

As soon as he turned back to look for Lloyd in the crowd his eyesight was blocked by glittery-red material, which barely covered the crotch of the woman standing before him.

"Get out the way!" Trigga said absentmindedly as his hand reached for his strip. He was annoyed at Luxe as she stood in front of him with one hand on her hip and the other twirling a long, curly lock of her hair.

"Dayum, you don't have to be so rude. A bitch just came by to check on you. I might have even given you a free lap dance if you'd been nice," she said darting her eyes to look at a dark-skinned, chubby man who was rushing across the room to help break up a fight between a stripper and a female.

Trigga recognized the lust in her eyes and she really was attractive with a big ole bubble butt, small breasts and cinnamon-complexioned skin. However, once again he admonished to himself that it was business before pleasure.

"Naw, I'm good, ma," he said standing up and then he moved her out of the way. He wanted to keep his eye on where Lloyd was heading.

"Shit!" he muttered when he realized that he had lost him in the thick crowd. He gently nudged pass Luxe, caught Mase's eyes and gestured for him to follow him. Again, Mase ignored him as a thick stripper bent all the way over touching her knees and making her ass cheeks thunder clap.

"Mase," Trigga said sternly walking towards him and grabbing him by his arm.

"Damn, nigga, you see this shit?" Mase asked. He nodded his head towards the woman in front of him when she was suddenly joined by Luxe, the stripper that had been trying to get Trigga's attention. The two women went at it slithering over each other's bodies like snakes in heat. All Trigga could do was frown at his brother and the chicks in contempt.

"Bro, I'm outta money lemme borrow another stack 'til later," Mase asked above the music as he grinned slyly, watching the dancers hump and grind on each other.

"Get da fuck outta here, nigga. You need to get on point. Fuck these bitches!" he shouted back at his brother as he bobbed his head trying to keep an eye out for Lloyd.

Mase and Trigga were fraternal twins, not identical. The only thing they had in common was that they were born on the same day. They even fought against that as Trigga waited until the absolute last minute to push through into the world. He was born at exactly 11:59:59 and from that day on, he'd managed to always be his own man and do his own thing without giving a fuck what anyone else thought.

Trigga was 6'5 with a bronze complexion and the sculptured, brawny physique of an athlete. He graduated from high school with high academic scores, he was also a gifted two sport athlete who played football and basketball, dominating both sports. He was offered scholarships from just about every prestigious college in the nation. He chose Duke University and was a sure prospect to turn professional. It wasn't until midway through the season in a game against Illinois State that Trigga went up for a dunk, shattering his knee. And there went his prospect for turning pro.

Mase was the complete opposite of his brother. Where Trigga was gangsta and deadly with a meticulous mind and chiseled, handsome features, Mase didn't have an athletic bone in his body. He had a large, bulbous nose with deep sunk in eyes that made him look sinister. The teeth he was born with were so severely crooked and gap-toothed that as a small child a dentist refused to work on them, saying that the boy would need a plastic surgeon not a dentist.

All throughout grammar school, Mase had unwillingly earned the nickname Shark Mouth and the girls found him unattractive. Even their mother favored Trigga, the more intelligent and handsome twin.

From birth, Mase came in the world a dark sheep and like all dark sheep he learned to play his role. Like, Trigga, Mase was also 6'5. He was a cool chocolate brown with brown eyes that matched his complexion exactly. He was covered in tattoos, giving him a roughneck, thug look. Some women found him attractive as long as he kept his mouth closed. Mase loved bitches and although they eyed Trigga first, Trigga was picky with who he laid with, letting Mase have his pick. Even still, Mase still envied Trigga in a lot of ways.

"Mase, we here for a fuckin' reason that don't involve you gettin' pussy right now," Trigga said through his teeth. "Did you see where the nigga went?"

"Listen, Trig," Mase said, finally turning his attention away from the broads in front of him. "This an easy one. The muthafucka's high and drunk as shit and his boys ain't even on point. We got the element of surprise on our side, just chill."

Trigga looked at his brother like he was crazy and willed himself not to smack the shit out of him when he pulled a wad of singles out of his pocket and started pouring them on the backs of the women who were trying their hardest to give him the best show. Luxe giggled as she reached out to grab his arm. Trigga batted her hand down and grumbled under his breath about how his brother wasn't shit.

Trigga pushed through the crowd as bouncers escorted two chicks out of the club who were kicking and thrashing in their arms to be let free, frantically searching again for Lloyd.

"Where the hell did this nigga go?" he asked himself as he rooted through the crowd. The smell of sweat, ass and liquor stung his nostrils as he walked in the direction he had seen Lloyd traveling.

"Hey!" a woman yelled out when he accidentally stepped on her foot. She turned around and glared at him with her nose twisted up, but when her eyes settled on his face, her expression softened immediately.

"My bad," Trigga mumbled as he continued walking pass her. She reached out to touch his face and he grabbed her hand gently. "Naw, I'm good, ma."

Swishing her long blond hair out of the way, the caramel-colored woman shot him a flirtatious smile that begged him to stay. Trigga pursed his lips and continued onward as he caught a glimpse of the back of Lloyd's head a few yards ahead of him at the bar.

FIVE

"So you done came back here to work, huh? What happened to the 'I'm getting my life together to be a college girl' bullshit you was talking a couple weeks back?" Lloyd snapped in Keisha's face as she leaned on the bar counter and swayed to the music.

Whatever Tish had put into that drink was making her feel good as hell, but at the same time uneasy as she glanced over her shoulder and saw Lloyd's crew still wildin' out and throwing money as Nicki Minaj's joint, *Truffle Butter* pounded through the speakers.

When she had first seen Lloyd walk in the club with all his hooligans it felt like her heart was about to leap out of her throat. She thought about creeping out the back door as she hid her face behind a drink menu. One of the last times she saw him was a memory she wanted to forget. Not only had he broken her heart, but he had humiliated her with his bitch of a wife, Dior.

Once the alcohol kicked in, she was starting not to give a care in the world about what Lloyd was up to. She had known that she would eventually run into Lloyd at the club. *Pink Lips* was where he did his business. He paid Cash a lot of money to be able to run drugs through his establishment and to let him and his East Point crew come in strapped with bangers, so he frequented the club often. Keisha just had been hoping he wouldn't be there during her first day back on the job.

"Hello? You hear me, Keesh?" he yelled snapping his fingers in her face.

Screwing up her face into a frown, Keisha pushed up off the counter and glared at him.

"Listen, don't be putting your fuckin' hands in my face!" she shouted. "I'm not your girl, remember that? Save that shit for your *wife*!"

Keisha eyed Lloyd angrily as his eyes bore into her face. As she stared, she saw his expression change and she instantly felt a lump forming in her throat. The emotion removed from Lloyd's eyes and it was replaced by a cold, deathly stare, which told Keisha that she was coming very close to crossing a line that she did not want to cross.

"Get your ass in the back and put on some fuckin' clothes," Lloyd demanded as he took in her attire. Then he stared at her haircut and Keisha could tell he liked it from the hint of desire that flashed in his eyes.

"Yo', you coming with me tonight and I don't want you in that shit." He pointed at her clothes with his head. She was wearing some cut-off jean booty shorts and a black corset top. It was cute, but left nothing at all to the imagination, which was exactly what Cash had requested.

"Hell, no," Keisha declared, snapping her neck. "Not gonna happen."

Baring his teeth and glaring at her with cold eyes, Lloyd reached over and grabbed Keisha by the arm, pulling her over the bar counter. His shirt raised up and she could see the chrome plated banger tucked in his pants.

"You must want me to beat your dumb ass in front of all these fuckin' people, huh?"

He threatened her as she stared wide-eyed into his sinister eyes. "I'll tell you what's going to happen. You're going to listen to what the fuck I'm telling you to—"

Just then out of the blue Trigga walked up and chest-bumped Lloyd causing him to spin around and reach for his banger. At the same exact time Trigga reached for his strap in his pants and opened his mouth to speak with deadly intent as the two of them stood toe-to-toe. It was about to jump off in a major way with gunplay as Keisha stood in the middle. She suddenly had the urge to pee; she was petrified.

"Yo, is he bothering you?" Trigga walked up and asked.

He towered at least four full inches over Lloyd who looked up at him like, 'Where da fuck this tall lanky nigga come from?' It would have been comical if it wasn't for the seriousness of the situation.

"Nigga, you betta take your Captain Save-a-Hoe ass outta here 'fore you get wet da fuck up," Lloyd said in a menacing tone.

"No! No! Everything is okay!" Keisha screeched with fear in her voice as she threw up both hands.

"Back off, nigga," Trigga spat at Lloyd with a sneer.

Lloyd opened his mouth to respond, then for no apparent reason, he crinkled his brow and did a second take at Trigga as if he recognized him from someplace. Keisha took a timid step back and rubbed the spot on her arm that Lloyd had grabbed. She stole a glance at Trigga.

Gotdamn, his tall ass is fine as hell!! she thought for a quick second. *He must be crazy as hell too.*

Like Lloyd, he was the type of nigga who walked in a room and instantly got the respect of everyone around. Everyone except Lloyd that was. He was the boss and this was his city. He didn't bow to no man. But for some reason, Lloyd backed up and smirked with a gloating grin that sent shivers down Keisha's spine. Her gut instincts were telling her that something was wrong, terribly wrong.

And she was right. If only she would have listened to the voices in her head telling her to get out of the club and get away from both goons. But she didn't because she couldn't. She was attracted to handsome thugs, the glitzy lifestyle; yes, the allure of gunplay even, as long as she wasn't involved. It was the lifestyle.

Keisha just happened to glance down at Lloyd's right hand and saw his fingers stretching, coiling and recoiling as if he was anxious to reach for his strap and just start shooting as he moved away. Trigga was standing tall, his chin jutted out at Lloyd.

Annoyed slightly at the small scene that they were creating, Trigga ran his tongue along his top row of pearly white teeth. He was ready to be done with the night and get back to New York. It would be a while before he took another job with his brother. Something just wasn't right about this situation and he couldn't put his finger on it.

"Aye, aye!" a voice yelled out from behind Keisha.

Ripping her eyes slowly away from where Lloyd was standing glowering at Trigga, she saw Cash as he ran over to the two men with his fat arms waving in the air. His chubby legs were moving fast, although his motion seemed so slow. Stopping at the side of the two men who continued staring each other down, he paused for a minute to catch his breath before speaking again.

"Listen, I'm askin' y'all to handle this shit *outside* my club. Black," Cash said looking at Lloyd. "You know that I'm always here fo' whateva you need, right? I don't want no heat comin' to my spot. Please," Cash pleaded as he continued with his labored breathing.

Lloyd clenched his teeth together as he continued to eye Trigga, his eyes black as his skin and clouded over with the cold anger that radiated from him. Suddenly, Lloyd grinned slightly, showing off his row of gold teeth to Trigga who still had a blank, stoic expression on his face, and backed away.

"I'mma get you later, my nigga," Lloyd promised Trigga as he walked away.

"Yes, later," Cash breathed out with relief as he wiped the sweat from his brow. "Whew!" He sighed. He'd dodged a big bullet.

Lloyd never backed away from anyone so he considered himself lucky that he had chosen this moment to do something he'd never done before.

The music started back and the strippers jumped back on the pole. Everyone went back to dancing and laughing as if everything was normal.

Trigga shook his head as his eyes shifted over to Mase who was still partying as if nothing had happened. He had his hands in the air and was grinding against a stripper as he waved a blunt in the air.

"Hey," a soft voice called out to him.

Trigga turned and looked right into the hazel eyes of Keisha who was giving him a small smirk. Looking at her, he had to admit that she was a beautiful woman, but that didn't mean much. He'd seen many beautiful women in his life. And all of them gave him the same look she was giving him.

It was something about the ego of fine ass women that made them go after a nigga who wasn't concerned with pussy. Sure, he got some ass every now and then, but it was only from women who already knew what was up. Women like the one in front of him would pretend to be fine with it for a short while and then start whining about going out and relationships. He didn't have time for that shit. He'd take a quick fuck, but that was all he had time for.

"Yeah?" Trigga answered her with a slight frown.

"Thanks for that. I appreciate it," she told him.

Trigga nodded his head only halfway paying attention to her. Without waiting for her to continue the conversation, he walked away and left her staring at the back of his head as he walked back to his spot in V.I.P.

SIX

"WHAT THE FUCK?!" Keisha yelled as she looked down at the 26-inch chrome wheels on her silver Mercedes Benz G550 SUV.

The driver's side tire was flat as a pancake. Upon further inspection Keisha saw two big ass holes in it. Someone had flattened her tire deliberately and she had an idea who.

"Got damn it! So this muthafucka had one of his bitch ass niggas flatten my muthafuckin' tires so I could go home with his ass," Keisha fumed as she stared at her tire.

Well, if he thinks I'mma ask his ass for help, he got another thing comin', she thought.

Tucking the brown knapsack under her arm that she'd purchased after Cash told her to dress 'less rich', Keisha turned around and stormed back to the club.

Every time I take two steps forward, I get knocked ten fuckin' steps back.

***

Shaking his head, Trigga walked forward and returned his eyes back to Lloyd who was saying his final two words to the stripper, Luxe, who had been trying to get his attention. She had finally been able to succeed in her plans to capture the attention of a man who had enough bread to gain her affection. From the looks of it, Lloyd was about to land a lot more than a lap dance that night.

As Trigga watched on, he saw Lloyd trace a line with his forefinger from her shoulder all the way down to the inside band of the tight, pink sweatpants that she had changed into. Luxe flashed him a sexy smile and wrapped her arms around his neck, pulling him into a tight hug as he grabbed her ass cheeks tightly and grinded her into him.

"C'mon, nigga. I ain't got time for this shit right here," Trigga grumbled under his breath.

And where the fuck is Mase? he thought to himself with annoyance. Both of them had gotten paid half up front for this job, but Mase was nowhere to be found when it was time to work.

"Hey," Keisha said as she turned to him, finally noticing his presence beside her. He was still looking over her head intently at Lloyd, but at the sound of her voice, he lowered his eyes to her face. Trigga's eyes softened a little once he focused on her, but she could tell by the serious expression on his face that his thoughts were elsewhere.

"I'm sorry…and I mean, I know this is way out of line, but I need a favor from you," Keisha said with a small smile as she tried her hardest to read the expression on Trigga's face while he stared at her blankly.

When he didn't respond, she cleared her throat to continue, "So I don't want to bore you with some long ass sob story, but you helped me once and I was hoping...."

As Keisha began to chatter on about her problems, Trigga's attention focused back on Lloyd who was moving towards his brand new gold Bugatti.

Show time, Trigga thought to himself as he watched. It was almost time to get to work.

Before Lloyd could pull off, Luxe walked back over to him, making him pop back out of the car again to say a few words to him. Involuntarily, Trigga's body went rigid as he resisted the overwhelming urge to casually walk over to dude and just calmly splatter his brains out with one shot to the dome with his .9 MM and walk off. That was normally his method of procedure, with the element of surprise in his favor.

Instantly, his mind went to stalker mode. Lloyd was the prey and he was the predator.

"Hello, are you okay?" asked Keisha innocently as she shivered against the cold night.

There was a light chill in the air. A full moon hung low, illuminating a cluster of bright stars. She gazed over at Lloyd as he entertained a stripper that she knew was named Luxe and then forced her eyes to turn away from him trying to ignore the both of them along with the sudden pang she'd felt in her heart.

"Yea, yea, I'm good," Trigga said and tore his eyes away from his soon to be victim.

Under his gaze, she shuffled her feet nervously with a slight pout and her delicate bottom lip stuck out. That's when he noticed the sexy dimples in her cheeks as she folded her arms over her ample breasts. There was something so familiar about her, but he just couldn't put his finger on it.

For a fleeting second, he contemplated whether he should ask her what she had been talking about, but he knew it would get him caught up in a conversation that he didn't have time to have. Normally he tried to keep women out his face when he was working, but there was something about her that enchanted him like no other chick he had encountered in a while. Maybe it was the 'good girl' innocence he could see in her, but it was something he wasn't used to in his line of business.

Without saying another word to her, he forced his eyes to look away from her in search of Lloyd. Several club patrons walked out of the club as Trigga bobbed his head trying keep his eye on the soon to be victim. The gorgeous chick before him with the bangin' body was standing so close that he could smell her perfume co-mingling in the air with the potent scent of loud that somebody was smoking in the parking lot.

He couldn't help but to steal another glance at her as he tried to keep an eye on dude. She seemed to be impatiently waiting for something as his mind raced. She was bad to death; bowlegged, thick thighs and ass for days in them tight jeans with the face of an angel.

Suddenly, Trigga saw movement out of the corner of his eye and it pulled his attention away from Keisha who was still standing in front of him with her wide, hazel eyes fixated on his face. Lloyd was pulling out of the parking lot.

"So can you or not?" Keisha asked him as he walked away from her towards his car.

"Yeah," he said over his shoulder, without thinking.

He took off walking in a brisk pace and glanced next to him, surprised to hear the patter of Keisha's feet following him as he waved through the congested parking lot. People who had left the club had brought the party outside.

Trigga shook off the confusion he felt as Keisha struggled to make her much shorter legs keep up with his long, slender ones. He had to focus. The vic was getting away.

He hopped into his whip as he watched the halogen lights of Lloyd's Bulgatti pull out of the entrance. Keisha ran over to the passenger side of his freshly waxed 2015 silver Audi R8, after seeing the license plate that read *Trigga.* She assumed that was his nickname. She pulled open the door and hopped in just as Trigga turned on the engine and slammed the car in reverse. Once she got in his whip she was immediately smacked in the face with the strong stench of weed, but she wouldn't dare speak on it.

"The fuck you doing in here?" Trigga yelled, looking at her wide-eyed as she struggled to get her seatbelt on while still holding her large bag in front of her.

"You said you would give me a ride home," Keisha replied quietly. Her eyebrows furrowed as she searched his face.

Is this nigga crazy? she thought to herself as she looked at his clueless expression.

"I said what?" Trigga asked her, but then noticed that Lloyd was pulling out. There was no time to waste. He had to get the job done. Without looking behind him, he backed the car out at max speed and turned towards the exit of the club.

Keisha gasped slightly as he maneuvered through the parking lot at top speed, "You said you would give me a ride," she spat out again quickly, trying to calm the vigorous beating of her heart in her chest.

"Well, I got some business to take care of first. It won't take long," Trigga responded like his thoughts were elsewhere as he shifted the car into drive and sped off.

He wasn't really paying Keisha the slightest attention at the moment. He knew he needed to worry about what he was going to do with her after he handled Lloyd, but he could only focus on one thing at a time. He would have to deal with that other shit later.

Keisha stole a glance at him as he focused on the road ahead of them. There was something about his demeanor that intrigued her, but it also irked her. Most dudes would have been all over her trying to impress her with attention and admiration, but not this dude. He was different.

At the same time, she wasn't sure that she wanted attention from another man who was obviously a thug. She was still dealing with the effects of messing with Lloyd. From the looks of Trigga, he was probably a drug dealer too. He had a nice ass car and bling that looked like it cost a grip. Dealing with him most likely wouldn't have been the best for her at the moment, but she couldn't help the way he seemed to captivate her.

"Okay are you going to ask me for my address?" she inquired as he pulled out into the street and punched the accelerator down so hard her neck snapped back as the car jetted forward. The Audi went from zero to 60 in what felt like 5 seconds as he sped through the light traffic in and out of lanes.

"What's your address?" he finally asked as he ran a red light.

Keisha's hand instinctively groped for the seatbelt again as he sped through the traffic like they had been shot out of a rocket. Eyes wide with fret, she exclaimed as he ran the second light.

"Uh, huh! You need to slow this damn car down!"

He ignored her and turned a corner on McDonald Boulevard, which just happened to be not too far from where she lived.

Instantly, the car slowed down, to her relief, as she watched him scan the neighborhood in search of something. This area was becoming one of the most violent sections of Atlanta. Just recently there had been a home invasion and a mother and her eight year old daughter had been robbed, brutally raped and murdered. Keisha hated living in such a bad area, but at the moment, it was all she could afford.

Suddenly, Trigga banged his hand on the steering wheel causing her to jump uncomfortably as he cursed in frustration.

"Fuck! That bitch ass nigga got away!"

Keisha turned and glowered at him as the Audi did a slow creep up the street. He was still scanning every car and building.

"You know what? You can let me out right here. I don't know what you got going on," she said half-serious as she watched him intensely.

An oncoming car-light illuminated his handsome face. His grey eyes held hers for a brief moment when he turned and looked at her like it was his first time realizing that she was there. Again she couldn't help thinking there was something about him that fascinated her. She wondered what he was up to, with his sexy self and them damn eyes.

Finally he expelled a deep sigh as he held on to the steering wheel so tight his knuckles paled when he asked with grit in his voice, "What did you say your address was again?"

She gave him her address. He pulled up his GPS on the car's navigation screen and that's when she noticed his banger wedged between his seat and the middle console. Although she instantly felt the alarm building in her chest, she played it off. It wasn't her first time around a street dude, and she had even dated a few dope boys prior to Lloyd. She was familiar with that lifestyle, the whips, and the money, even the guns. Although for some strange reason she found herself attracted to a few rough neck thugs, she had sworn to only deal with good boys after Lloyd. However, something about Trigga was different and made her question that decision.

She turned in her seat,   trying her best to relax in the leathery comforts of his ride as the car sat idle and he punched in her address in his GPS system. She couldn't help staring at the amber glow of the countenance of his handsome face.

"Oh and by the way, Mr. Indy 500 Speed Racer Driver-Man, my name is Keisha," she sassed sarcastically with the hint of a smirk.

Trigga's eyes snatched up and focused on her face showcasing all of the humor one would have at a funeral and it made Keisha regret her lame joke. Then suddenly his eyes softened and he chuckled, suppressing a laugh, or maybe it was a grunt? It was hard for her to tell in the limpid light of the mysterious night.

"I can tell from the way you was holdin' that seatbelt over there that you got a mean grip. So I'mma drive yo' feisty ass home before you choke the shit outta me," he joked. Keisha blushed under her buttery cheeks at him poking fun at her.

Looking at the side profile of his handsome face she then added, on a kinder note, as she tried to elicit a conversation from him to get a better vibe, "You never did tell me your name."

Her words were as soft as a whisper and she tried to smile, but her checks wouldn't oblige.

Silence.

Thoughts merged in her head as she waited. He was still looking for something and whatever it was had him vexed. Then he spoke without even looking at her after he had put her information into his GPS system.

"You can call me Trigga," he said in a strained voice and placed the car in gear again. He started to drive slowly with his eyes still ablaze with whatever it was he had been searching for.

"Trigga… humph…" she repeated quizzically. His name naturally rolled off her tongue as she shifted in the cushiony leather seats.

"So…" Keisha continued with her feminine curiosity getting the better of her. "Are you from Atlanta?"

"I look like an Atlanta nigga to you?"

"Not really…but what you tryin' to say about Atlanta niggas?" Keisha asked faking an attitude as she sucked her teeth at him.

Trigga glanced at her out the side of his eyes and smirked. "We both know that's not the question you really wanna ask me." He turned his attention back to the window.

Keisha studied his handsome features some more without him noticing as he continued to stare out the window into the darkness. He had a mystique about him that fascinated her. He was right. That wasn't what she really wanted to ask him. She wanted to know if they could go somewhere other than her home so she could find out more about him. Once she was able to gather up the courage to ask, she opened her mouth to inquire about his plans for the rest of the night.

Then suddenly the car stopped so fast that it screeched to a halt. He reached for his banger. He was focused on something moving in the darkness. Something she couldn't see.

She could feel the hair rise on the back of her neck when she spoke, "Wh… What's wrong—" she was about to say when he stopped her.

"Shhhh!!" he hissed to silence her and thrust his arm forward, shoving her back against the seat.

The banger was in his other hand locked and loaded as her heart began to pound in her chest like a bass drum. She sat perfectly still with his arm across her breasts as she nervously struggled to breathe by taking several sips of air like she was drinking through a straw.

The moment lulled as the suspense built. She sat perfectly still as a mannequin in a store and forced her eyes to focus out the driver's window at what Trigga was looking at.

Then her vision cleared as she blinked her eyes several times at what looked like gloomy fog outside of the car. She saw the silhouette emerge and to her utter surprise she recognized who the shadow was. It was Lloyd. He was walking away from his Bugatti and was fast approaching them.

Instantly, the first thought that occurred to her was Trigga was about to bum rush dude over what happened at the club. That would have been good had she been a hood chick and she was down for violence, but Keisha was the complete opposite. She didn't have the stomach for violence and blood, especially something that started over her.

She had to stop him.

"Don't do that, it's only a misunderstanding at the club," she said with a plea in her voice. She gripped his arm just as he reached for the car door handle, but he shook her off.

Just then, there was a tumultuous sound of loud glass shattering combined with Keisha's bloodcurdling scream as her passenger window burst, shattering and spraying her face with broken glass.

An armed gunman wearing a ski mask and toting a six shot Mossberg shotgun barked threateningly as he reached in and yanked her by her hair, placing the shotgun to her head.

"Fuck nigga, move and I'ma spray dis bitch brains all over the car with you next."

Trigga's hand was still on his banger and his heart was beating in his throat. In his peripheral he could see Lloyd in the dim of the night strutting over with three other dudes and he wasn't staggering anymore like he was drunk. It was then that it dawned on Trigga that them Atlanta niggaz was a lot smarter than he thought.

Trigga had blundered severely in the worst way and fell for the oldest trick in the book: a set-up.

"Bitch ass nigga, now what!" Lloyd growled outside of the driver's side window fogging it with his breath as three of his goons stood by his side wearing hoodies that partially concealed their faces. One of them was carrying a banger at his side.

One of the goons opened the driver door and grabbed Trigga by his shirt to pull him out. He lashed out and started throwing punches as the man fought back ferociously, landing punches to his face and neck.

Think fast! Think fast! Trigga's mind churned as he was being pulled from the car.

Being a product of the streets, he knew the law of street wars. It was better to have an all-out shoot-out with a chance to survive, than to just give up to be taken hostage at the mercy of your enemy.

With no other recourse as he was being pulled from his vehicle, he reached down for his piece and came up firing. The big 9.MM exploded, illuminating the night with what looked like orange balls of fire as Keisha's piercing screams pierced through his ears.

BLOCKA! BLOCKA! BLOCKA! BLOCKA!

BOOM! BOOM! BLOOM! BLOOM!

A barrage of gunfire exploded and the car rocked. Trigga was hit multiple times, riddled with bullets as he was able to get off a few shots, killing the gunman holding the shotgun. Then he turned to the assailant that had been pulling his shirt and pummeling him with blows and shot him in the head, causing it to explode like a grapefruit. Blood splashed Trigga's face as the melee continued.

The man holding Keisha's hair tugged hard, nearly ripping her hair from the scalp. Keisha grunted as her neck retched upwards while he brought back the shotgun to her head and pressed it further into her skull. The strength of his grip on her hair ripped her eyes open and she looked at her assailant.

Her eyes focused on something shiny peeking out from under the black bandana he wore around his neck. A large, gold cross medallion slid from under the black material and on it was Jesus nailed to the cross. Keisha's eyes teared up as she looked at it, praying that Jesus would be with her now.

As Trigga tousled with more of Lloyd's goons, he felt his strength failing him, but he gritted his teeth and continued on as much as he could. Just as he was about to raise his piece to fire a shot into the skull of the dude in front of him, more shots rang out from close range beside him. Then the most eerie thing happened. Keisha stopped screaming. She went silent. She wasn't moving.

Things went from bad to worse.

Eyes mired with one of his assailant's blood and partially blinded, the rancid smell of sulfur emanated. Trigga could almost hear death beckoning to his spirit as his blood leaked from his body.

Through his bloody eyelids, he saw Lloyd raise his gun. He manage to duck in a nick of time as the gun Lloyd had exploded, barely missing his head and only taking off a piece of his right ear. Trigga was able to raise his banger and fired at close range at Lloyd, his attacker.

Click! Click! Click!

With horror, he realized his gun was empty!

SEVEN

With a gloating grin, Trigga's victim turned victor. Lloyd placed his 44. Desert Eagle inside the car as several bodies lay on the worn pavement. One of the gunmen lay in front of the car struggling to get up. Trigga's entire life flashed before his eyes as the feel of the cold steel pressed against his forehead.

Death would come soon.

With grit in his voice and breathing heavy in a raspy tone, Lloyd intoned, "Pussy nigga, you fell for the oldest trick in the book. How they gone send a fuck nigga to murk me when I run this shit?" Lloyd cocked the gun and continued. "How about this...I collect the mill on my head from that Queen bitch and use your body as mine."

Lloyd began to laugh a dry cackle as Trigga felt his body grow weaker. He didn't have a clue as to what he was talking about and didn't care. It was either die, or fight back while dying.

All of a sudden, Trigga punched the accelerator, the Audi jetted forward as the tires burnt rubber while Lloyd, caught by surprise, held on to the car window.

There was a gruesome thump as the car leaped forward hurdling over one of the wounded gunmen that had been lying in the street trying to get up. The gunman's belt buckle caught on something underneath the car penning him underneath the car as Lloyd held on for dear life. The foreign car sped through the night, reaching speeds of nearly one hundred twenty miles per hour as Lloyd yelled for Trigga to pull the car over.

Out of pure malice, Trigga drove with reckless abandonment. He was bleeding badly and going in and out of consciousness as the panic stricken Lloyd continued yelling and screaming in his ear like a bitch for him to stop the speeding car.

Up ahead, Trigga spotted a lone white van parked on the side of the street. He gunned the engine faster and faster like a Kamikaze gangster heading straight for it. He intended to kill his attacker in the cruelest way.

Just in a nick of time as the Audi sped for the van, Lloyd let go of the car barely escaping death. The sound of twisted metal collided horrifically in a sonic boom that resonated. The body that had been unmercifully dragged underneath Trigga's vehicle was somehow jarred loose upon the impact and lay in the street. He sped off leaving a carnage of bodies in his wake and Lloyd laying in the middle of the street, lucky to be alive.

*****

Bright lights and salty sweat co-mingling with blood stung Trigga's eyes as he drove recklessly, drifting in and out of oncoming traffic. The front bumper of his car occasionally scraped the ground, knocking sparks from it. There was a puddle of his own blood in the driver's seat, saturating it with red. At the time he had no way of knowing that he had been shot over seven times.

For some reason the ringing in his ears wouldn't stop as he squinted his eyes at the ardent lights, his vision blurred. He wiped his face with a bloody hand and felt a small piece of his ear was missing as he looked over at the girl lying motionless in his passenger's seat.

"Ohhh, God. Fuck!" he groaned and reached out to take her bloody wrist in his hand while swerving to avoid hitting an upcoming garbage truck. She had no pulse.

She's dead? he thought dreadfully as he attempted to look at her and drive haphazardly.

There was so much blood, gory blood, covering the beautiful girl's face. It looked like she had been dipped in a pool of red paint. From somewhere in the car, the chick's phone rang. He wasn't sure where it was exactly.

Then a thought occurred to him, a thought that sent a timorous chill down his spine. He was in foreign territory so to speak. This was not his city, not his place. In fact, he didn't know a soul and he had just left a slew of bodies behind him. If the dead girl was discovered in his whip it would just be more bodies, more time, more difficult to explain to the authorities if he was pulled over. He was a black dude, which meant under America's cardinal rule: guilty until proven innocent.

He needed to get to a hospital. He needed to get help, but first he needed to get rid of the dead girl in his vehicle.

****

On a desolated street in Decatur on the south side of Atlanta, notorious for drugs and violence, Trigga drove with the bumper dragging the ground. He passed a group of homeless people burning a fire in a trash can to keep warm and that's when he spotted it: a huge dumpster up ahead. He had a bright idea, he could dump the girl's body there.

He pulled the car to the side of the street and sat trying to gather his wits. By then, the pain was excruciating. The bright lights engulfed his vehicle. He looked up and there was a cop car headed straight for him. He dared not move; that might get the cops' attention. For some reason, he held his breath and glanced over at the dead girl.

"Fuck!" he scuffed begrudgingly and slid down in the seat as far as he could go and for the first time in Trigga's adult life, he did something he hadn't done in a long time.

He prayed.

"God, please, don't let these crackas get me."

The cops were using their patrol car search light; its strong beam was bright as the sun as it bounced off each car and headed straight for his whip.

The light streaked across his face as the patrol car passed and continued moving. Absentmindedly, Trigga expelled a deep breath he didn't realize he had been holding as his hand caressed a bullet-hole in his chest. He was still leaking blood profusely.

He strained to exit the vehicle and the pain was unbearable. To his surprise, the city had got bone-chilling cold as he hobbled to the passenger side of the car, leaving a trail of blood dripping from his pants' leg. He reached inside for the dead girl as he looked around. He hoisted her up and her neck fell back. A car passed with loud rap music playing, so he stood perfectly still. As soon as the car was out of sight, he made his move.

Walking fast, he staggered and almost fell with the girl, because it felt like she weighed a ton. As he reached the dumpster and positioned his body to toss her in, the girl moved and moaned softly. Trigga almost shit in his pants.

"Wha-da-fuck?!" he screeched befuddled. His arms were weary. He was fatigued and losing too much blood. Maybe it was his imagination playing tricks on him. He shook her softly in his arms causing her head to sway from side to side.

Nothing.

Then disgruntled voices droned, echoing like he was standing in a tunnel.

"Hey!! You! What you doing to that lady?"

Trigga looked up with his hands soiled with blood and a possibly dead Keisha in his arms as several homeless people that had been huddled around a fire were approaching him fast. One of them had what looked like a bat, or a two-by-four in his hand as he walked briskly with a purpose.

Trigga's first thought was to drop the girl on the pavement and take off for his whip, but her body felt warm in his arms. The fact was, he wasn't sure if she was dead or alive. And if she was alive, he couldn't leave her.

Turning around, he took off for his vehicle and was met by the homeless people. One of them had on an Eskimo jacket with a fur hoody that looked weather worn in the night chill, all he could see was a dark face in the hoody. Next to him was what he thought was a rotund short dude that he later realized was a lady. She had on a wool coat that looked two sizes too big, she was also carrying a bat. There were several other homeless people standing in the backdrop.

"Man, whu'cha doin?" the dude with the Eskimo coat asked as he approached.

Trigga didn't answer as he struggled awkwardly to open the door with a bloody hand and hold the girl at the same time, his meager strength was waning, and he was starting to see stars. He was about to pass out and lose consciousness.

Somebody gasped. "God lawd!! They both covered in blood. Jesus lawd help'em!"

Somebody started quoting bible verses as Trigga placed Keisha back in the car. He shut the door and turned, but his strength left him. He fell to one knee.

The woman with the bat shirked, "Awe help 'em Jesus! Help him lawd." She took off and began to pace as she threw up both her hands like an evangelist in a church. The bat in her hand hit the worn pavement in a thump.

Then suddenly Trigga felt hands, lot of hands. The homeless people were helping him to his feet.

"We gone call an ambulance. We gone get y'all some help. My wife and I is preachers; servants of da lawd," the homeless man who was wearing the Eskimo coat said. His teeth were rotten and there was a fetid odor coming from his body like he hadn't bathed in weeks, months perhaps.

Somehow Trigga managed to push off the man and got back into his car with his vision blurred. He turned the engine and heard somebody say, "Ask him can we borrow five dollar for he leave."

Just as Trigga was about to pull off, the guy with the Eskimo coat ducked his head in the car and said as he gestured pointed with a gloved hand with the fingers cut out.

"If you go straight ahead till you see that light on Peachtree make a right it will take you to the Decatur hospital on Memorial Drive".

Trigga nodded his head and put the car in drive. For some reason he glanced over at the girl and resisted the urge to check her pulse again. One thing was for certain, if she was dead she was as beautiful in death as she was in life. He couldn't help it, he caressed her bloody cheek and felt a piece of glass on her skin. Her body was warm.

The homeless man asked, "Bro, can you spare five dollars—"

Trigga drove off in the night trying to remember the directions the homeless man had given him as he went in and out of consciousness. Miraculously, he found the hospital up ahead carved out in gray granite stone with its huge majestic archways and glaring lights that read, 'GRADY HOSPITAL."

He parked the car, not even turning off the engine and dragged himself out then lumbered over to the passenger door leaving a trail of blood as he panted and struggled to breathe.

As he reached for Keisha, there was a whooshing sound that caused him to look up. It was the mechanical hospital doors opening as several people walked out. One of them was a medic, a white male in his early 20's. He looked hankered and wary like he had a long night and it was the end of his shift.

Trigga staggered, for some reason the bright hospital lights felt like they were blinding him. His first instincts were to get help for Keisha then dip. He wasn't no fool. The authorities would tie him to her body if she was dead now, or died later.

As the medic walked by with a small throng of people across the parking lot Trigga turned his back as the other people passed him and then timed the medic just as he approached

"I need your help!" Trigga said. To his surprise, the medic jumped back and gasped.

"Good Lord!" he exclaimed. The fitted cap he had on his head nearly fell off as he moved away, startled.

"Bu…buddy, you look like you need help bad," the medic said as he looked at Trigga covered in blood.

"It's not for me, it's for her." Trigga gestured as he pointed inside the car. The medic's eyebrow formed an arch across his forehead like a tight line when he looked inside the car and asked, "Is she breathing?"

Before Trigga could answer, he slightly staggered, then fell backwards on his back against the car and slid down on his backside. His body was depleted of energy due to the fact he was bleeding internally and hemorrhaging blood from a punctured lung. He was dying.

Trigga could vaguely hear the medic frantically yelling into his hand held radio, but then he passed out. The last thought on his mind was a prayer for Keisha.

He prayed that she didn't die.

EIGHT

Three days later…

Trigga woke to the constant chatter of voices and a glaring, luminous white light. In the distance he could barely make out the episodic beeps that chimed incessantly from the EKG machine connected to his body. A tube had been implanted in his nose that ran down his throat into his chest. He was in bad condition. After being shot seven times he had lost a considerable amount of blood and had to receive a blood transfusion. His body was hooked up to a life support system.

Trigga was barely able to open one eye and even though he had been heavily medicated before going into surgery and after, he was still in immense pain. He had suffered seven gunshot wounds, had a ruptured lung repaired and three broken ribs attended to. One bullet tore off a piece of his ear and had to be surgically repaired.

He could barely make out the figure in the room towering over him in the bed. It was his older brother Mase. He was in a heated argument with a plain-clothes detective. Alcohol and the potent smell of Loud permeated the hospital room.

"Man, I don't give a fuck. Dats my little brother and we ain't even from here."

"That doesn't matter, we have reason to believe your brother was involved in a triple homicide and there's possibly a fourth victim here in the hospital fighting for her life," the detective said.

His name was Detective Lewis Burns. He was dressed nicely in a beige suit and tie sporting a brown brimmed fedora hat that matched his attire. His partner, Detective James West, was rather obese with hound dog eyes, a double chin and a pot belly. He too was dressed to a T in a gray suit and shiny Stacy Adams shoes as he stood over by the window.

"So, what, you gone arrest him?" Mase asked.

"No, we can't do that because he might just be a witness to the crime. We need to know what happened to the car and possible weapon that was in it," the cop said with steel in his voice in an attempt to intimidate Mase.

Mase made a face and said, "Man, how many times I'm going to tell you? I brought them to the hospital in my car."

"And how many times am I going to tell you the medic said that was not the car they arrived in? And your brother's hands tested positive for gun residue, which means he fired a gun."

"That don't mean shit! So what he fired a gun?" Mase responded angrily back. "This Georgia…don't y'all country ass white folks fight for errybody to have a gun down here?"

Detective West was agile for a man his size. In three quick strides he was all in Mase's face. He talked slow, but deliberate.

"We can charge you with obstruction of justice, conspiracy to impede the investigation of a murder and a list of other charges. We ain't stupid, we know you moved that car and all the incriminating evidence that was inside of it. We also know your brother fired a gun. We have an eyewitness that is in a coma. If she wakes up and says he had something to do with it you and your brother's ass is grass, so I suggest you save us the trouble and start talking."

Mase took a step back at that. He was a little bit rattled by the threats, but for him there was no turning back. He rolled his shoulders with a shrug, reached in his pocket, removed a partially burned Black and Mild cigar and then feigned a confidence that he really wasn't feeling.

However, he had watched too many hours of *The First 48* and had a remedy for the situation when he said, "Man, dats my little brotha. I ain't telling y'all shit on him. I don't wanna talk no more. I am requesting my lawyer be present for any further questions."

Mase then searched for the cigarette lighter in his pocket and pulled it out. He was surprised to see his hand shaking when he tried to fire up the Black and Mild.

Detective West knocked the lighter out his hand and gave him a shove. Burns, his partner, quickly stepped in between the two.

"Fuck you do that fo?!" Mase asked with a contemptuous scowl as he held the bent cigar between his fingers. "I just bought this shit!"

"No smoking in here, asshole! But I'm telling you this, I'ma smoke your *ass* if we find that car with your prints on it! Or better yet, when that young lady wakes up and we hear her side of the story, somebody's going away for a long time."

"Do your job!" Mase said with a wave of his hand.

The other detective, Burns, walked up, reached into his suit coat and tried to pass Mase his card.

"Give me a call if you change your mind."

"Fuck outta here!" Mase said pushing the card away.

The cop placed the card on the bed next to Trigga. Both detectives exited the room, leaving Mase alone with the terrible sound of his brother's breathing apparatus and the horrible EKG machine droning on in synergism with the constant murmur of hospital noises.

"Ho… ho… how… did… you… find me?" Trigga managed to croak in a painful, dry voice once he saw the detectives leave. His lips were cracked and dry. There was a bandage wrapped around his head from where he had been shot in the ear.

Mase looked up, startled, as he did a double take over at his brother and said with apprehension in his voice, "Nigga, you can hear me?!"

Trigga nodded his head 'yes'. "Nigga, you just got done shouting in my damn ear. If I was dead, yo' loud ass would have woke a nigga up."

"They just lettin' you get visitors today…yo' ass is banged up. You been out fo' three damn days—"

Trigga wiped his lips with a dry tongue and muttered barely audible, "The girl... did she make it? Is she alive... I need 'ta know."

"I dunno, but they callin' her a witness. Do she know anything, bro?"

Silence was loud, other than the noises coming from the machine and the constant whir of the hospital's P.A system.

"You should have waited for me, bro. You should have never tried to take dude out alone."

"I had him, but somebody set me up... I walked into an ambush..." Trigga groaned and pressed his lips tightly together as he winced in pain.

"What you mean somebody set you up?!" Mase raised his voice.

"I followed him to the other side of town...Him and his boys was waiting on me... Just when he was about to shoot me in the head he said something about collecting the million dollars and getting back at Queen...I don't know who told him about that shit."

Mase flinched like he had just been doused with a bucket of cold water at what his brother said.

"I...I don't know what that shit is about," Mase quickly declared. "But if that bitch that was in the car with you saw anything, from the way the cops was talking about using her as a witness, you know we gone have to whack her ass. Right now they only think they got is some gunpowder on your hands. But if she is alive and she talks, it's the death penalty for you with a triple homicide."

"I dunno man… sumptin' isn't right…" Trigga said feeling groggy as he began to nod off again.

"Yea, what ain't right is that bitch. If she is still alive I'ma make sure she don't make it to the cops to testify," Mase said with a grin, happy to see his brother close his eyes.

Trigga didn't answer because he couldn't. The inertia of drugs had him sedated. He fell back into a deep sleep and dreamed about Keisha; the pretty bloody girl that was in the car with him when the shooting started.

He murmured in his head for Mase not to touch a hair on her head. She was his angel…the reason he was alive. He'd only gone to the hospital to save her life and ended up getting his own life saved as well. He needed to see her again. But Mase had his own reason for wanting to kill Keisha and it had nothing to do with his brother.

NINE

Keisha stirred awake as the mechanical beeping grew louder and louder in her head. She wanted to open her eyes, but it was proving to be difficult as the throbbing in her head became stronger and stronger.

The fuck happened to me? she thought to herself.

As she struggled to open her eyes, her nose caught a whiff of the pungent smell of bleach and disinfectant. When her eyes opened like tiny slits, they were assaulted by the blinding lights above her.

"Wha—"

She tried to speak, but was stopped by the feel of something in her mouth. It was a feeding tube. Keisha's eyes widened as she looked at her body, strapped down on a bed that felt about as comfortable as a cardboard box. She had tubes coming from everywhere it seemed; her mouth, her arms and even between her legs. She couldn't move, couldn't sit up. She wasn't sure what was going on, but she could tell that she was in a hospital.

Blinking back tears that were forming in the corners of her eyes, Keisha fought a mental battle to remember what had happened to get her there. Had she been in an accident?

As her eyes flicked out of the window to her right, she saw a man walking by. Even before she knew why, she felt her heartbeat quicken and a tremor move through her body from the icy feeling of fear that crept down her spine.

I know him, she thought as she looked at the man.

His brown eyes were filled with murderous intent as he angrily passed by. He had a low hair-cut, dark brown skin and a muscular physique. He was wearing a simple white tee and had a gold diamond earring in his ear.

The club, she thought to herself as she suddenly remembered where she had recognized him from. He'd been one of the only people to order drinks from her then she remembered he was also the guy looking at her in the shadows while she was standing outside.

Almost at the exact moment that she recognized him he turned towards her. They instantly locked eyes and his dark brown ones were on her hazel ones. She watched in silence as the corners of his lips turned up into what looked like a smile, but she couldn't really decide because it didn't look kind-hearted, but evil instead. As he pressed his face up against the window, something fell from the neck of his white shirt. A gold Jesus-piece.

Keisha's eyes focused on it for a minute as she tried to remember why the piece seemed so significant to her. She felt fear overcome her as she looked at it, but she didn't know why. What she did know, from the feeling of panic that was overtaking her body and the snarl and cold, dead eyes on the face of the man in front of her, was that he was not a friend.

Instantly, her eyes frantically darted around the room for an emergency button as she began to hyperventilate. She struggled to breathe as he moved to open the door to her room. She found it at the bottom of the remote on the small wooden table next to her and pressed the button down firmly as Mase walked in.

"Hey sexy, you remember me?" Mase asked in a menacing tone as he looked around suspiciously and squinted down at her body. She was badly bruised and in excruciating pain. She had suffered three gunshot wounds and was miraculously lucky to be alive. A portion of the right side of her head was shaved for the stitches that had been placed there.

"I see you're awake and out of the ICU now," he said with grit in his voice.

Keisha said nothing as she watched him approach, and was suddenly completely consumed by terror. She watched him with wide-eyes as he approached her and prayed that someone would enter her room. From behind him, she saw nurses and visitors walking back and forth down the hall, but not one of them was paying attention to what was going on in her room. Looking back at the man before her, Keisha saw the outline of something bulging out from his side and instantly knew that it must have been a banger. He was strapped and ready to finish the job he'd started.

"What's wrong? You not afraid are you?" he asked her.

Just when she had built up the courage to scream, she heard a voice that she would never forget. It was the voice of someone saving her right in the nick of time.

"Hellooo? Did you call for— Oh, Ms. O'Neal! Honey, you're finally awake! Praise God!" someone said from behind Mase.

Surprised, he flinched like he had been caught in the act of something. His hand gestured for his strap as he backed out of the way when an older black woman dressed in baby blue scrubs walked over to Keisha's side holding a clipboard. She was oblivious to what was happening as she began to check the machine next to her while she smacked her lips. Keisha still feared the worst as the nurse checked something on the screen of the beeping machine next to her and scribbled on the clipboard. Mase continued to stare daggers at her.

Turning to Mase, she said, "Sir, I'm so sorry, but I'mma have to ask you to leave for a bit. The doctor will need to come in and speak to Ms. O'Neal and we have to run a few tests. Are you immediate family?" The elderly woman scrunched up her nose as she peered at Mase over her large eyeglasses.

Mase hesitated as he continued to look between the nurse and Keisha. He looked as if he was ready to start blasting. Then suddenly something washed over his face and he smiled as he backed away and said barely in a whisper, but still in a menacing tone,

"No… I'm not a family member…Just a friend," he lied as he continued to look at Keisha. The older woman nodded and waited kindly for him to leave.

As soon as he was gone Keisha let out a deep sigh. Her body was shaking visibly as the nurse continued to check her vitals.

"Okay, it looks like we may be able to get these tubes out right away! You're one lucky child. You suffered a gunshot wound to your head that just barely grazed it. A fraction of an inch from where it hit and the bullet would have entered the frontal lobe of your brain. We did a MRI and everything came back negative…"

Keisha tried to focus in on her cheerful mocha-colored face, but her thoughts were on the man who had just left and there was no doubt in her mind that he had come by to harm her. The woman's voice droned on in the background of Keisha's thoughts while she removed the feeding tube, causing her mild discomfort.

But why? she asked herself as her heart continued to pound in her chest like a bass drum.

Then a chill crept up her spine as she began to remember other details from the night before. Trigga…the man who had given her a ride from the club. They had been attacked.

Was he dead?!

She sat straight up in bed with her eyes spread wide and still focused on the door as she asked in a high pitched tone that caused the nurse to turn and look at her with alarm.

"Where is he?"

"Honey, I don't know, but he said he would come back soon," the nurse responded and gently caressed her arm, thinking she was talking about the guy that had just walked out the room.

Keisha picked up on it and corrected the nurse. She pulled her arm away.

"Not him, the dude that was in the car with me when the shooting occurred. Is he still alive?" She heard the quiver in her own voice and hugged herself. She feared for the worst.

The nurse gave her a grim expression with a shrug as she rolled her shoulders.

"Yes, he's alive. The police sure want to talk to you and I think it has something to do with him. He's down the hall and was in critical condition—room 714. He was shot multiple times like you but last I heard, he was still in a coma. He lost a lot of blood. But both of y'all have been doin' better. It's like y'all either got the best of luck or a guardian angel watchin' you," the nurse blurted out as she tended to Keisha's bandages.

The silence was loud as merging thoughts evaporating, consumed with daunting fear and dread. For Keisha, it was the fear of the unknown. She still couldn't quite remember everything from the incident that had happened to land her in the hospital and it was bothering her.

The nurse added in a somber tone. "I notice you ain't had no family, or loved ones come visit… except this one girl. She came for a bit on the first day and then stopped."

"What girl?" Keisha asked as she absent-mindedly mopped at the bald spot on her head with her hand.

"I don't know. Can't remember what she said her name was," the nurse responded.

Still silence followed awkwardly.

"I don't mean to get in your business, but if that's your boyfriend I can go check on him. Although I'm not assigned to him I can find out if he's okay if you want me to," the nurse offered without making eye contact.

Keisha responded with a tacit nod as she nibbled on her bottom lip and thought about Trigga, the phantom gangsta that she didn't know.

He had caused her so much pain and anguish already and they'd barely met. She pinched her eyes closed and felt a tear cascade down her cheek as she absentmindedly rubbed again on the bald spot on her head and felt the grisly forty-eight stitches.

Then she opened her eyes and asked, "How long do I have to be here? I wanna go home." Her voiced cracked with emotion.

Just then, as if on cue, a doctor walked in. He was a short Asian man with black hair and a perpetual smile. He introduced himself to her with a smile, but Keisha's mind was elsewhere, so she barely heard a thing. The entire time he spoke to her as he shined a light in her eyes. He continued to smile as he examined her with nimble fingers and hands as soft as a female's.

Afterwards, he said in broken English that was hard to understand, "N' dee mornin' you free'ta go. Do you have healthcare, or some type of insurance?" His last sentence came out perfectly clear like he had rehearsed it millions of times. He was still smiling.

"Yes, I do," Keisha lied.

The doctor examined the stitches and staples in her head and removed the tubes from her body, which were connected to the machine. He then went on to explain her injures in words she couldn't quite understand. However, he did try to explain to her that the area in her brain where she had suffered her injury was also the part of the brain responsible for memory. For a time she may have a problem with that, but it should clear up soon. She'd banged her head pretty hard but her injuries were pretty minor. She was lucky because it could have been worse. It felt like worse.

The doctor agreed to give her a prescription and painkillers. Then he and the nurse walked out leaving her alone with her riveting thoughts.

****

Keisha lay in bed wide awake listing to the constant murmur of hospital noises and the voices in her head as she pondered over the events that led up to this tragic moment. Then something suddenly occurred to her. Something that she hadn't remembered. How could she have forgotten? Trigga had been following her ex, Lloyd. What was that all about? Then the shooting had started.

"Seven fourteen!" she blurted out loud as she suddenly remembered what the nurse had said. That was the hospital room Trigga was in down the hall.

She rose from her bed too fast and quickly felt nauseated from a pounding in her head. As she held on to the hospital bed railing with rubbery legs, she put on a new hospital gown and slippers. She walked into the small restroom to relieve herself and was startled at what she saw in the mirror. The right side of her face was swollen and bruised. The grisly extent of her injuries was evident and there was a deep purplish gash under her eye.

As she stared at her reflection in the mirror, , examining herself with her short hair standing straight up, she choked out a sob that segued into a soft cry as she fought the battle of her emotions.

She managed to pull herself away from the mirror and staggered back into the hospital room. There she was confronted with doom. One large looming figure hovered above her and she recognized the person instantly.

"Where do you think you're goin'?"

Crippled by fear, Keisha's legs suddenly went wobbly and she nearly fainted.

TEN

"Lloyd!" Keisha yelled out. She stared into his callous brown eyes as he stared down at her.

She felt an icy chill slowly creep up her spine while she looked at him. She didn't know what to think. The last time that she'd seen him, Trigga was chasing him down and it led to them being trapped right in the middle of a shoot-out. And someone was trying to kill her. Did Lloyd have anything to do with that?

"Keesh...you're up," he said as his eyes raked her body.

Although she was wearing her hospital gown, she felt vulnerable and naked under his intense stare. His eyes came back up to her face and he sat silently for a moment as he took in her bruises. Keisha teetered a little from side to side as he examined her face, because she felt self-conscious about her injuries.

"Yes," she said quietly as she continued to look at him. He stood silently with his eyes trained on her face, then finally his serious expression broke and he exhaled heavily.

"Damn, Keesh. I'm happy as hell that you straight," he said as he sat down in the chair behind him. "Shit, I don't know what I would do if you got hurt."

Keisha stared at him with a crease in her brow as she started to think about what he was saying.

"That night...the shooting. You mean you tried to kill me," she whispered as she narrowed her eyes and gripped the front of her gown in an attempt to hide her body from beneath. Even in Lloyd's relax state, he still had a threatening demeanor about him and she still wasn't exactly positive that she was safe. She moved slowly towards the emergency button, hoping that he didn't notice her intent.

"Nah, man. That nigga you was with...Trigga, he bad news, ma. He ain't nothing but a dope boy outta New York who out here tryin' to play in my city. He came down here sayin' he wanted to buy some good shit. I had my men send him some shit and he popped them niggas off real quick and now he tryna haul ass to New York without givin' me my bread."

Keisha just stared at him blankly, not fully believing what he was saying. Trigga hadn't seemed like the type to do some shady shit like that. Granted, she didn't know much about him, but she could tell that he wasn't the type of nigga to do some sheisty shit like Lloyd was claiming.

Noting the skepticism in her eyes, Lloyd changed up his angle. "You just got caught up in the middle of some shit that didn't concern you, shawty. You know I'mma street nigga, so I settle my scores in the streets. I recognized him the club so I was 'bout to handle his ass that night. I ain't even know you was in his whip. The fuck was you doin' in there anyway? You fuckin' that nigga?" Lloyd asked as he looked at her with suspicion in his eyes.

Keisha's angry expression waned and shame filled her eyes as she pondered his question. It was as if they were back in a relationship and she had been caught with another nigga. Lloyd was extremely jealous when it came to her and now, knowing that she had been in the car with one of his enemies, she didn't know what he would do.

"I—uh…I just met him that night. I didn't—" Suddenly, something occurred to her. "Wait…nigga, we ain't together! You kicked me out and went back to your *wife*, remember that?"

Before she could say another word, Lloyd jumped up so fast that the wind from his motion caused a few papers the nurse had left to fall from the table by her bed. He came in so close to her that she sucked in a breath as a reflex from him suddenly invading her personal space.

Grabbing her by the chin, he pulled her face up and looked her square in the eye, saying, "Listen, Keesh. I don't give a fuck what happened between us before. I thought I lost you that night and I want you to come back, a'ight?"

Keisha goggled up at him with wide eyes as she listened to what he was saying. She had no words at all to say. How in the world could he go from being the asshole he had been the past month or so to now wanting to have her back in his life?

"Hell, no!" Keisha said as she pushed him away. Although she pushed with all of her might, Lloyd barely moved, but he did drop his hands to his side and took a small step back. "Get out...now."

"You don't want that," Lloyd said to her dismissively. He sat back down on the dark blue chair behind him and then leaned forward, placing his elbows on his knees as he looked at her.

"Listen," he continued. "I'm sorry for how all that shit went down with Dior, but you gotta see things from my prospective, ma. Dior had my back when I was down and we been through a lot of shit. She helped me get to where I'm at now. If somebody helped you achieve your dreams, would you say 'fuck you' to them even if you don't love them no more? It's a way I gotta go about this shit. I gotta do this shit the right way."

Keisha eyed him with a skeptical glare. "And the right way was throwing me out on my ass?"

"I didn't throw you out on your ass. Dior was threatening to take all my shit and leave. You know I can't let her do that. I asked you to leave and I gave you a rack of cash to start a new life. I know you don't deserve a nigga like me. You need you a nice lil' church boy," Lloyd joked with a grin. He knew damn well Keisha wasn't the "church boy" type of girl.

Trying to suppress a smile, Keisha snorted, but Lloyd knew he had found a small way in.

"Listen," he said as he stood up. "I want to take you out this shit. You look like you good to go. And I know this bullshit ass food they got here tastes like bricks. Lemme get you home and take care of you, ma," Lloyd told her with pleading eyes.

Quietly, Keisha thought about what he was saying. Honestly, she did want to leave and she had nowhere to go. On top of that, she could guarantee that Cash probably wouldn't be too eager to offer her the bartending job back once she told him that she would need a few days off to get herself together after already not showing up for three days. She had flaked on him once again and it would be impossible to get him to forgive her.

"Ooookaaaaayyyy," Keisha eased out reluctantly. She had a feeling that she was agreeing to do the absolute wrong thing, but she couldn't think of anything else to do. She had nowhere to go and no one to call.

Lloyd jumped up and swooped her into his arms, lifting her feet off the ground as he hugged her tight. She groaned and pushed him away, although she had missed the affection.

"C'mon…damn. I'm still sore as hell."

"My bad," Lloyd said with a grin and placed her on the floor. "Let's get your stuff and get you out of here." He started looking through the cabinets and drawers around the room for her belongings that the hospital staff had wrapped up. Finally he found a small plastic bag with her clothes and purse wrapped up in it. Opening the bag, he pulled out her purse and left everything else.

"Wait, what about my clothes?" Keisha asked him. She looked down at the wrinkled up hospital gown she was wearing and the large fleece socks they had put on her feet.

"Forget that shit. I'mma take you shopping and get your hair did. I'mma make my shawty look real nice so you know that a nigga ain't playing no games. Let's go." Lloyd winked at her and held out his hand for hers. She was about to place hers in his when she remembered something.

"Wait!" she said as she pulled away from him. "Someone came in here and I think he was trying to kill me. A guy…tall, dark-skinned, dark eyes…" Lloyd stared at her with a confused expression on his face. She ran through her memory for something else that could describe the man. "Oh, he had a gold earring in his ear…and a chain around his neck. A Jesus piece!"

Under her desperate stare as she tried to tell him who it was, Lloyd's expression switched instantly and he looked like a light went off in his head. Before answering, she watched as he thought for a few seconds longer before responding to her.

"You saw him at the club, right?" Lloyd asked her then waited for her to respond. Keisha nodded her head. "Prolly somebody sent by that nigga, Trigga, I told you he was a dangerous muthafucka and you need to stay away from him. You a liability because you saw too much. Let me handle him."

Keisha clamped her mouth shut and thought back to that night in the club. She had seen him speaking with that same guy a few times, but it didn't seem like they were friends so she hadn't thought much about it. Something seemed odd though and it had something to do with that Jesus piece, but she couldn't quite place where else she'd seen it other than in the room that day.

But why would Trigga want me dead?

As if knowing her thoughts, Lloyd answered her question for her. "He was tryin' to off your ass to protect Trigga, or some shit. Might of found out me and you used to be together and thought you had set him up or some shit…I don't know, but I do know that those niggas can't be trusted. I wanna protect ya shawty."

Keisha swallowed the lump in her throat as she listened to Lloyd explain everything to her. It was obvious that Trigga was a dangerous man and she could tell that right when she first met his gaze. He had a threatening aura about him and his stance and demeanor commanded the attention and respect of everyone in the room. Lloyd was right. She had to stay away from him. If he knew that she had a past with Lloyd there was no way he wouldn't suspect that she had something to do with him getting shot.

"Okay," she said finally. "Let's go."

Lloyd held out his hand to her and she grabbed it. They were about to walk out of the room when she stopped.

"Wait," she said.

"Damn, what now?" Lloyd sighed as he turned to her. "We gotta get out of here before the doc, or somebody come back."

"I need to make a call. You go to the car and pull it up front. I'll be out in a minute."

Lloyd hesitated for a moment as if he wanted to tell her no, but then he exhaled loudly and ran his hand over his low-cut hair.

"A'ight. Hurry up."

Keisha nodded and watched him leave. Once she saw him get on the elevator, she ducked out of the room and started walking as quickly as she could down the hall to room 714. Part of her was saying that she needed to listen to Lloyd and leave because Trigga was exactly who Lloyd said he was. He probably wanted her dead, but the other part of her knew that Lloyd had lied to her many times before and she needed to investigate for herself.

ELEVEN

As soon as Lloyd stepped into his brand spanking new black on black Ferrari convertible, he grabbed his iPhone and called the last number in his call log. Cranking up the engine, he turned on the air and sat back in the seat, enjoying a reprieve from the hot and humid Georgia air.

"Yo," the voice said on the other line.

"Aye, nigga, I got that shit handled," Lloyd said as he slowly pulled out of his parking space and around to the front of the hospital entrance.

"Already? Damn, nigga, you don't play no muhfuckin' games!"

"Hell, naw. What the fuck you thought? I know them New York niggas might not be gettin' no pussy where you and ya lil bro from, but down here us country boys can scoop up a bitch quick," Lloyd laughed. The person on the other line joined in on the laughter before his tone turned serious.

"Man, I'm just mad as hell that I ain't know the bitch was still alive all this time. She coulda been handle days ago, my nigga."

"Yeah, I ain't know she was alive either after that night. Thought we only had one loose end. But I don't want you to kill her tho'. Shawty might come in handy," Lloyd thought as he stroked his beard.

"A'ight, but you know this shit can go bad if anything goes wrong, right?"

Lloyd tried to quench his anger as it rose in his throat, but it was proving to be difficult. He wasn't used to niggas questioning his word. Gritting his teeth, he let out a long breath before he responded.

"Mase, listen my nigga, I don't know what you think this is, but I ain't brand new to this shit. I got shawty on lock. She ain't gone do shit I don't tell her to. You just take care of your loose end that's still alive when the muhfucka supposed to be dead," Lloyd fumed.

When Mase came to him over a month ago, he told Lloyd some news that he needed to hear. Queen, the head of the infamous *Queen's Cartel*, a drug organization out of New York City, had a hit out on his life. One thing he knew about Queen was that she was a bitch with the mind of a boss nigga. She was as ruthless as they came and she didn't take shit from anyone. She would cut off her own right hand if it was a threat to her empire. He didn't know how she had got to be that way, but he didn't care. All he knew was that he needed to stay the hell out of her way.

One of Lloyd's top men, Sergio, told him one day about some dope boys out of Virginia who had some shit that the streets were craving. Sergio told him that he could get it for him on the low.

Lloyd went for it; he trusted Sergio and gave him the okay to check everything out without investigating it himself. At the time, he was dealing with shit from Dior being pregnant and was trying to hide Keisha, so he was preoccupied and figured if he couldn't trust his team, there was no point in having one.

Unfortunately that was the wrong move. Sergio robbed the niggas of the dope and killed them all, thinking that they were some small time hustlers. When Sergio was found a few days later dead in his own backyard, killed execution style with his hands hog-tied behind his back and one bullet straight through the dome, Lloyd became aware from an icy note left at the scene that the men that he'd killed belonged to the Queen's Cartel and one was Queen's own brother.

Lloyd had thought with Sergio dead that Queen was satisfied, but he should have known that she wasn't. She was known for fully extinguishing the line of whoever had wronged her. She didn't leave no stone unturned and he was next in line to be dealt with. When Mase came with the news of what Queen was planning and told him that she'd hired him and his brother, Trigga, to do the dirty work, Lloyd had been ready to off that nigga on the spot, but Mase had an ulterior plan.

"This is how this is gonna go," Mase had said as he held the gun to Lloyd's head.

Lloyd felt the ice-cold barrel pressed against his skull, but it didn't scare him at all. He was infuriated that he had been caught slipping. How the hell a nigga he didn't even know had been able to just waltz his ass right up to Lloyd as he was taking a piss in the bathroom of the Pink Lips was beyond him.

Where the fuck is Kenyon? *Lloyd thought as he waited for Mase's next words.*

Kenyon had seemed preoccupied the entire night. It was bad enough that he had been acting funny ever since the incident with Dior and Keisha. Lloyd thought back to that day when he saw him and Dior in the car talking with their heads bent down close together. For a split second he'd thought something was going on with the two, but he knew that Dior wouldn't try him like that. No matter what the hell he did, she wasn't that stupid.

"You listenin' nigga?" Mase asked him, pushing the gun further into his skull.

Lloyd gritted his teeth as he moved his hand to his side slowly, reaching for his burner.

"You don't wanna do that. I got some shit that you need to hear," Mase said. "And if you work with me and not against me, I can help you make a whole lot of money." Then he told him the entire story about how Queen had hired him and Trigga to kill him.

"Damn, I knew that shit," Lloyd muttered as he thought about what Mase had said. "I ain't even have nothing to do with that bullshit scheme Sergio pulled."

Even as he said it, he knew it didn't matter to Queen.

"I know you didn't," Mase said to him. "That's why I'm gonna present you with an offer. I got a way to get at Queen and all her money and dope, but I need yo' nigga to help me. I need a team.

Let's kill Trigga, I'll swap his body for yours and deliver it to Queen. Then I'll help you get at Queen. Then we'll split the dough and go our separate ways."

Lloyd scrunched up his face at the wall at Mase's words. Something didn't sound right.

"Man, don't you live with that nigga? Why can't you just off his ass in his sleep or some shit? And can't you use any nigga body to swap wit' mine?"

"I want him dead, but I don't want his blood on my hands," Mase said. "You help me and I'll help you. You could take over the whole east coast and more."

Lloyd mulled the idea around in his mind for a minute, but it wasn't like he had a choice. Mase had the gun to his head, so if he didn't agree to the deal, he wouldn't make it out. He would die in the bathroom of the strip club with his dick hanging out of his pants.

"A'ight," he agreed.

Mase lowered the gun and they discussed business. Then he followed Lloyd out of the club to his car where they exchanged numbers and plotted their plan. Once they got outside, Lloyd finally saw Kenyon, huddled off alone in the corner talking on his phone.

This nigga cakin' with some bitch while I had a fuckin' gun to my head, *Lloyd thought as he walked to his car.* I'll deal with him later.

After finishing up the conversation with Mase, Lloyd watched him drive away with a menacing stare on his face.

He didn't trust anything about Mase and as soon as Trigga was dead and Mase helped him get at Queen, Lloyd was planning on putting a bullet through him too.

"If you can kill your own blood, there ain't shit about you that can be trusted," Lloyd said to himself once he got off the phone with Mase. He couldn't wait until everything was done with Trigga. If he didn't have police standing outside of his door, Lloyd would have tried to finish him off while he was in the hospital.

"Shit," he muttered to himself in frustration.

Just as he looked towards the doors of the hospital, he saw Keisha emerging, holding the open part of her hospital gown closed. He'd never seen her look so bad since the moment he had first met her in the strip club. She looked like a pack of elephants had done the A-town stomp all up and down her ass. She was bruised all over her face. Her caramel skin-tone was muddled with purple, red, black and blue. She was hideous.

The last thing he wanted to do was play nurse and caring pretend boyfriend to some crazy bitch who had pulled a gun on him. Looking at her in the hospital gown with half her head shaved, she already looked like she had one foot in the loony bin. Now he had to put up with her for a little while longer.

Truth was, he didn't care about killing her, but he didn't want her dead just yet. If anyone could make a nigga be caught slipping, it was a bitch. Though he couldn't be sure, he had a feeling that he might be able to use Keisha later on down the line to get at Trigga. In addition to that, he needed to keep her close to make sure she kept her mouth shut in the meantime. Only way to do that was to get her back on his team until they killed Trigga. Then she would go next.

Lloyd watched her as she fumbled with the door handle with her face screwed up in concentration.

"Ah, shit," he said, jumping out of the car to get her door for her.

"Thanks," Keisha said with a small smile as she allowed him to open her door and help her inside. Something was bothering her; Lloyd didn't know what and he didn't want to ask. He'd done enough chitchatting to last him a lifetime.

"A'ight, I'mma take you to the crib, let you clean up. Then you can put on one of my shirts and some basketball shorts or something until I come back with some clothes and shoes so I can take you shopping," Lloyd said as he pulled out of the parking lot.

Silently nodding her head, Keisha leaned her head on the window and delved into her own thoughts.

***

"I got they asses," Dior said as she watched Lloyd and Keisha pull out of the parking lot of Grady Hospital.

She pulled off behind them and trailed Lloyd's car as he drove, dipping in and out of traffic. He was a crazy driver and hard to keep up with, but she'd had years of practice when it came to following him while he had a bitch riding shotgun.

After following him for a few more minutes, Dior exhaled sharply and turned around to go in the opposite direction. She already knew where Lloyd was going. He was driving straight to his little love-nest, his downtown condo. This one was different from the one she had found Keisha in over a month ago. He didn't think that she knew about this one, but she did. He was smart, but she was smarter, especially when it came to busting his ass in the middle of cheating and he kept forgetting that.

When Dior pulled into the driveway of the modest 3,500 square foot home with a beautifully landscaped lawn and 5-car garage for Kenyon's expensive cars, she parked, silenced the engine and walked up to the door as if she lived there. She might as well; she'd pretty much been at his house every minute that she wasn't at home. Which, with Lloyd spending more and more time working on some top-secret mission with some new business partner from New York City, was pretty much all day and even some of the night.

Before she could even put the key Kenyon had given her into the lock, he pulled open the door and she was greeted by all of his sexiness. He had his head covered with a skully and was wearing only a white tee with some black sweatpants and $4500 custom-made Giuseppe sneakers. He was effortlessly sexy and Dior felt her treasure box down under filling up with something she was all too eager to give to him right away. But first, she had to handle business.

After kissing her deeply on the lips, Kenyon stepped out of the way to allow her to pass. Dior walked into his home, making sure to rake her fingertips across his washboard abs as she waltzed by.

"He's with her again," Dior said finally once Kenyon closed the door.

"Who?" he asked her a slight smile spreading on his face as he walked her straight to the kitchen. He loved a woman who had an appetite with no shame.

He walked slowly towards where she stood in the kitchen making herself a plate of the food he had on the counter. It was Popeye's chicken, biscuits and red beans and rice; her favorite ever since she'd hit her third trimester. Greasy and fattening, yes, but she couldn't get enough.

"Keisha. The bitch I caught him with over a month back. I knew he wouldn't be able to keep his dick clean. I've been following his ass for days because I knew he was up to something. All these damn hushed conversations outside and behind closed doors. That nigga ain't as slick as he think he is," Dior fumed, stuffing a piece of hot, greasy chicken between her rose colored lips.

Kenyon nodded his head, deep in thought. He couldn't get over how stupid Lloyd was. He had everything he could ever ask for in Dior and still he couldn't help but fuck around. Over the past month Kenyon had fallen in love with Dior and wanted her to himself. He was tired of ducking and dodging a nigga who didn't even appreciate her.

"What you gonna do?" he asked her, still watching her eat. He moved towards her and grabbed a plate off the counter. She stopped him, popping the top of his hand with her delicate fingertips.

"I'll make your plate baby," she cooed softly.

Kenyon grabbed her ass and squeezed it tightly. He loved everything about Dior and couldn't wait to take her clothes off after she was done eating. The only thing that matched her large appetite was her sex drive. She ended each meal with a nice serving of his dick. She couldn't get enough and he couldn't give her enough.

"Anyways," she continued. "I know last week, I told you I just wanted to off his ass and get it over with, but I said that out of anger more than anything," Dior said.

"He still checkin' in on you every day?"

"Try every fuckin' hour. This shit has gotten to be ridiculous. He's been doin' his shit for so long that now his paranoid ass thinks that I'm doin' dirt too. He makes me call him every damn hour to tell him where the hell I'm at. And I'm scared to lie to him because one time I told him I was at Publix and the muthafucka showed up there to see!" Dior sighed. "I don't want to kill him, but I gotta be done with his ass. This isn't how I want to raise my daughter."

Kenyon nodded his head sharply as he looked at her. When Dior had said, while standing in her large grand formal living room, that she wanted to devise a plan to kill Lloyd and rob him of his money and dope, he had listened as he always did when she ranted about her marriage to Lloyd. He'd even agreed to help her when she'd asked because he figured she was bullshittin'—or at least he hoped so. She was pregnant and bout to bust, so every day she was saying something crazy out her mouth. But as much as he wanted her, he couldn't allow her to kill his cousin. The nigga wasn't shit, but he was blood after all.

Dior continued, "I don't wanna do no crazy shit because, after all, Lloyd is going to be Karisma's daddy." She rubbed her stomach softly. "I don't want to do anything that might hurt my baby girl, then I want to take every fuckin' thing he owns. I mean *every fuckin' thing.*"

"Hmm," Kenyon said as he thought. "And then what about us?"

"Listen, after we take that nigga's shit, you and I can make our own empire somewhere else. You're the brains behind this shit anyways!" Dior pushed more food in her mouth and followed it up with a bottled water that was on the counter next to the food.

Kenyon nodded his head. He had more than enough money to take care of them both, but he knew that Dior wouldn't be satisfied until she had her revenge. Lloyd wouldn't get hurt in the process...nothing would be hurt except for his pride. But if he was the hustler Kenyon knew he was, his cousin would get back on top in no time. With this plan, Dior could have what she wanted and he could get what he wanted, too. Plus, Lloyd would get what he deserved.

"What we gotta do," Dior said. "Is find a way to use his own damn system and paranoia against his ass."

Kenyon nodded his head again and smiled at her.

"A'ight," he told her. "I'm in."

Dior smiled widely and wiped her mouth with her hand as Kenyon looked at her with lustful eyes.

"You ready for me to make your plate?" she asked him.

"Fuck the food," he told her.

He walked over to where she stood and grabbed her in his arms. Lifting her up as if she wasn't carrying a huge, bulging belly in front of her, Kenyon walked towards his bedroom holding what he considered his whole world in his arms; Dior and the baby he would raise as his own.

TWELVE

Keisha rolled over in the large, plush King-size bed in the master bedroom of Lloyd's new condo and pulled the red, silk sheets up underneath her chin. She was comfortable, clean and should have been relaxed, but something didn't feel right. She looked around the dark room which was only illuminated by the dim lighting provided by the setting sun and thought about the story Lloyd had told her back at the hospital a few days back.

I don't know, but I do know that those niggas can't be trusted. I wanna protect ya, shawty.

But Trigga didn't seem like the one who couldn't be trusted. Lloyd, on the other hand, had lied for over a year straight about a lot of things like it wasn't nothing. The vibe that she was getting from him now seemed odd too. The first few days, he was trying his best to be a gangster Prince Charming. Opening doors, getting her clothes…all the shit she would have loved for him to do when they were together but he'd never done. But his façade was fading and he was going back to the same old Lloyd she'd always known.

Keisha watched him from the bedroom as he opened up three black duffle bags of work on the table in the living room. He was facing her, but his attention was on the product and money. She studied his face as he concentrated on what was in front of him. She watched as he sliced open one bag and took a whiff then his phone rang.

Keisha closed her eyes and pretended to be sleeping, but through the tiny slits in her eyes she saw him flick his eyes towards the bedroom where she lay before answering the phone. In a hushed tone, he answered it as he walked out of the front door. Laying back on the pillows, Keisha looked at the ceiling and thought back once again to what had happened days before.

After Lloyd had left out of the hospital room, Keisha made a mad dash down to Trigga's room. In the back of her mind, the warning that Lloyd had given her was ringing, but the closer she got to room 714, the quieter the ringing became. The hall wasn't empty, but it was filled with nurses and doctors who seemed preoccupied with their own matters. No one was interested in the woman rushing down the hallway in a hospital gown, bruised face and an expression of desperation on her face.

As she turned the corner to where the sign told her Trigga's room would be, she almost ran smack into the nurse who had been in her room earlier.

"Oh my God! I'm so sorry, ma'am!" Keisha managed to get out though she was nearly out of breath.

"Oh, it's okay honey," the woman said with a smile. She winked at her and then said with a knowing look on her face, "You going to see your handsome friend down there, huh?"

Keisha swallowed hard and nodded her head. Feeling a bit self-conscious about her own appearance as the woman reminded her of how "handsome" Trigga was, she ran her fingers through her matted hair.

"Oh, you look beautiful darlin'! Stop fussin' with your hair. The officers are in there speaking with him, but they should be out soon and then you can have your private time with him. Now take it easy. You're doing well, but you're still healing."

Keisha nodded her thanks and the woman winked again before continuing her walk down the hall.

Swallowing hard, Keisha walked with trepidation and hesitancy towards Trigga's room. Through the glass windows, she could see the back of the two police officers who were speaking to him. Both white men who stood tall, had a militant and threatening presence about them. Slowing her stride to more of a stealthy creep, Keisha slowly peered inside through the slightly ajar door.

Although she'd tried to prepare herself mentally to see him, she couldn't help the gasp that escaped her lips once her eyes fell on his face.

He had a bandage around his ear that was stained pink with blood and needed to be changed. His face was bruised and his shirt was off, but his torso was wrapped with gauze. His body was hooked up to various machines that were set up around the room. His eyes were barely opened into narrow slits and his lips were dry and brittle. He was looking into the eyes of the detectives around him with defiance, annoyance and rage. Keisha felt the heat radiating from his stare even from where she stood and it made her shudder. It was a wonder that the detectives were able to stand so boldly before him.

"Miss, can I help you?"

A thin white woman with short blond hair and a cheerful smile appeared in front of Keisha suddenly with her hands on her thin hips. She cocked her head to the side as she stood happily in her pink and white scrubs, much too eager to assist. She must have been new on the job.

"Umm....no. I'm just waiting," Keisha answered her as she focused in on the woman's cheerful face. "That's my friend in there. I'm just checkin' in on him."

"Oh!" the woman exclaimed still holding on to her bright smile. "Well, I'm Sarah and I sit at the desk in the middle of the hall. If you need anything, give me a holler!"

Keisha nodded curtly at the woman and watched as she nearly skipped away down the hall in an obvious good mood.

At least someone is having a good day, *she thought.*

Remembering the reason for her current location, Keisha flicked her eyes back to Trigga's room and was surprised to see that his dark grey eyes were looking directly at her.

Keisha gasped and her own eyes opened wide with surprise as the chill of fear traveled up her spine. She was just about to dart back down the hall from where she'd come, but stopped when she noted Trigga's facial expression. The threatening glare that he'd been giving the detectives was gone. His eyes had softened and the fiery rage that was in them had been replaced by care and concern. Although her mind was telling her feet to move, she was held in place by his gaze which was almost beckoning for her to come inside. Her lips parted slightly as she stared back at him. Her feet shifted as she prepared to enter the room. Then she remembered the detectives who were in there with him, but it was too late.

Keisha turned to run back down the hall at the exact moment that Detective Burns snatched his neck around to see what had captured Trigga's attention.

"Ms. O'Neal!" he yelled out as he suddenly pivoted on his feet, looking directly at her.

"Going somewhere?" he asked in a deep baritone voice.

"I... I ...wasn't going anywhere," Keisha lied as she stopped in her tracks. Nervously, she asked a question that she'd already known the answer to, "Who are you?"

"Homicide detectives. I'm Lewis Burns and this is my partner James West." The cop gestured with his hand introducing his partner. Both of them were dressed nicely in suit in tie. The other detective, James West, held her with a piercing stare that made her feel uncomfortable.

"Ohh," was all she could think of as a response as she continued to hold on to her gown. She shifted uncomfortably on her

feet, casted a wary glance down at the floor, then stole a glance at Trigga. He frowned at her as he nodded his head, "NO".

Baffled she didn't know what to think as the homicide cop continued.

"You were involved in a triple homicide where people were murdered in cold blood. We would like to ask you some questions first. How do you two know each other?" Detective Burns asked as he took out a pen and small note pad from inside his suit coat breast pocket and began to walk towards her.

Keisha wasn't a hood chick, she just had a habit of dating hood niggaz with money, but she was no dummy either. In the hood, snitches had stopped getting stitches a long time ago and were getting free trips to the morgue, courtesy of a gunshot instead.

She clamped her lips tightly as she looked at Trigga's pathetic body laid out in the bed as he continued to adamantly nod his head, "No," a silent warning.

Finally, she mustered the courage to talk meekly as she fidgeted.

"I didn't see anything...my head was injured, so I can't remember. Don't know nothing...is it okay if I have my lawyer present?" Her voice quavered.

Both cops exchanged quizzical expressions and then Detective West stepped forward. He was a bear of a man who stood about six feet. He wore a trimmed beard with sagging jowls and deep socket eyes that appeared to be set too close together. She caught a whip of an odor of cigarettes and some type of musk cologne as he frowned at her. Keisha had seen men like him before and they all acted crazy.

"It's your right to have your lawyer present, but you're not being questioned as a suspect, only as a witness to a horrific crime. Your life might be in danger."

"No, I'd rather my lawyer be present either way... Sorry."

For some reason, Detective Burns got angry. "Have it your way. You have just gone from looking like a victim to a suspect and you're going to talk to us one way or the other even if I have to subpoena..."

"Man, fuckin' beat it! You see she don't wanna talk to you!" Trigga said causing both cops to whirl around to look at him.

"You watch your fuckin' mouth, 'cause as it is, you're on borrowed time. We are still waiting on more ballistic tests and forensic results to come back then one, if not both, of you are facing the death penalty," the burly cop, West said.

"Whateva, just do your job, cop!" Trigga said.

The detective moved towards Trigga like he was going to assault him, causing his partner to intervene, stepping between the two of them.

"Let's go," Detective Burns said tagging at his partner's arm and together the two of them brushed pass Keisha standing at the door. There was no doubt in anyone's mind. They would be back with arrest warrants.

"*Man, that was gangsta as fuck what you just did in not talking to the cops—*" Trigga was about to say before he was interrupted in a sharp, clipped tone.

"*Was it?!*" Keisha nearly yelled.

"*Why...what's wrong?*" Trigga asked in a strained voice as a P.A. system blared in the background.

"*I'm in the fucking hospital shot to pieces. I was in a coma and damn near dead. You barely escaped death and you're asking what's wrong! I fuckin' feel like you set me up or some shit.*"

"*Hold the fuck up, shawty. If anybody should be suspicious, it should be me of you.*"

"*Why?*" she shot back.

"*'Cause you asked me for a ride and I don't know you from the next bitch. Do you know how many niggaz get set up by a bitch when they be from out of town?*"

"*Bitch!?*" Keisha's voice screeched because she was instantly offended.

"*Naw ma, I'm not calling you a bitch I'm saying for an example.*"

"*An example, huh? Like how you and your niggas came to the A to rob and shoot people and steal their drugs?*" Keisha sassed catching him off guard, causing his month to form an incredulous O.

"*My niggas? Man, I ride solo and I don't rob another nigga for shit! Who da fuck told you that silly shit?*" Trigga asked suddenly and tried to sit up, but he winced noticeably in pain.

Keisha went silent. She didn't want to tell him that she knew Lloyd. It would only increase his suspicion of her.

"Look, I gotta go," she said suddenly and turned to leave.

"Wait," Trigga yelled out. She turned back to him. "If you gotta go, then that's cool, but put your number in my cell." He beckoned to his phone on the table next to him. "I'm not a bad nigga, I promise you. When I get out of here I'mma come lookin' for you, but in the meantime, you make sure to call me if something happens."

Keisha stared at him and could tell that he was telling the truth. She walked over to the table and pressed her number into his phone and called her cellphone, so she would have his number as well.

"I got it," she said and pursed her lips together as she looked at him on the bed. He stared at her so intently that she felt self-conscious and put her hand up to cover her bruised face.

"You beautiful yo," Trigga said. "I'mma find your ass when I get out."

Keisha smiled in spite of the situation and felt her cheeks go hot as he continued to look at her.

"Text a nigga or somethin'. I ain't even got cable in this room. I could use someone to talk to," Trigga said with a smile. She could tell he was trying to ease her mind.

Keisha backed away from his room and prayed that the flutters in her stomach meant that Trigga was someone who could be trusted and Lloyd just had it all wrong.

Brushing away the thoughts of Trigga and the detectives, Keisha shifted in the bed and tried to close her eyes to go back to sleep. Then her eyes shot open as she suddenly thought of something that she hadn't before. How could she have overlooked such an obvious detail?

The kind nurse who had tended to her told her that she'd only had one visitor in the three days she'd been in a coma in the hospital; a woman. Keisha had assumed that woman was Tish. She was the only one she could think of who would have come to see her. The nurse never mentioned a man coming to see her...not even once. But as soon as Mase had left out of Keisha's room, Lloyd had later showed up. How in the world did Lloyd know that she was awake? He just so happened to visit her minutes after she'd come out of a coma, although he'd never come around in the three days that she'd been there? Coincidences like that didn't just happen.

Keisha sat up in the bed and slid her long slender legs off the side. Placing only her pink pedicured toes on the mosaic tile floor, she stood up and crept slowly to the front door of the condo. She heard a murmur of sound as she approached, so she looked out of the peephole. It was Lloyd. He was standing right in front of the door still speaking on the phone.

Keisha placed her ear to the door, closed her eyes tightly and focused on listening intently.

"You sure that cold ass bitch's gonna trust you enough so we can get this shit done? I got my part of this shit handled. I just need you to do what the fuck you 'posed to do," Lloyd said to someone on the phone.

Keisha had no idea what he was talking about, but she kept listening anyways. This was something that she'd never done in the past. She knew that Lloyd didn't play about his business and if she overheard something he hadn't meant for her to know, it could lead to her paying the ultimate price. Lloyd's gun didn't have no loyalties when it came to his business. Anybody could get the breath snatched from their bodies if they put their noses where it didn't belong.

"Naw, nigga, I got this bitch handled. She don't eat and she don't shit unless I tell her to." Keisha's ears perked up at that even though she still had no idea who he was talking about. Was it Dior? "She was in the nigga car damn near dead and his dumb ass took her to the fuckin' hospital instead of chuckin' her ass on the side of the fuckin' street. The nigga had to know five-oh was gone be at his ass for that. I'mma use her to get that nigga since I can't trust your dumb ass to do shit right half the time."

Keisha sucked in a breath as she listened. Her heart started beating ferociously in her chest and her knees began shaking once it dawned on her what Lloyd was saying. Her instincts had been right. Lloyd could not be trusted and that's when she got further confirmation of his deadly intents.

"Mase! I'm tired of tellin' you the same shit over and fuckin' over. Handle your shit with Queen so we can get that bitch's empire. I got this over here handled…"

MASE! Keisha screamed in her thoughts. Lloyd was working *with* him. He wasn't Trigga's man, he was Lloyd's!

Instantly shards of her memory returned to her and her breath got caught up in her lungs as she recalled that one of the gunmen who fired shots at her had been wearing the exact same chain that she'd seen on Mase in the hospital. That's why her body had reacted the way it did when she saw it. Although her mind couldn't recall why at the time, she instinctively knew once she saw it that Mase couldn't be trusted. It was because he had been the one who had shot her in the car that night.

Covering her mouth with her hand to hush her heavy breathing, Keisha backed away from the door. She'd heard enough. Her eyes filled with tears as she tried to calm her thoughts enough to settle her reactions. She had to get back to the room and pretend that she hadn't heard a thing. It was the only way that she would be able to make it out of the condo alive. She needed to hide her revelation until Lloyd left out again.

Stepping back slowly from the door, Keisha knocked into something behind her and it sent a sharp pain through her back. She felt the object teeter from the force of the hit and she turned quickly to grab the object before it fell, causing a noise loud enough to alert Lloyd of her position at the door. She grabbed out in the darkness and her hands clutched around one of the arms of the coat rack just in time to keep it from falling. But then the door opened behind her.

Whooshing around with tears still in her eyes, Keisha came face to face with Lloyd. His dark brown eyes were filled with surprise as he stared silently at her. Then a flicker of something passed through them and they went black as he pulled his lips tight into a sneer, exposing only his bottom row of gold teeth. Noting his hand as it moved to his waist where he had his piece stashed, Keisha's body started shaking violently with fear as she looked at him. Her teeth chattered so hard and loud that it was the only sound that could be heard in the darkness as the realization of everything set on her.

This was the end.

THIRTEEN

"Da fuck you doin' Keesh?" Lloyd growled as his dark face twisted up in a sneer.

Keisha's eyes darted back and forth in the small foyer and her feet shifted slightly as she tried to think of something—anything that she could tell him. Something that would make sense.

"I—I…" her voice croaked as she started and winced slightly at her inability to keep it together under Lloyd's glare.

"What, Keesh?" he asked, a little calmer but Keisha wasn't fooled. She saw his hand inching towards his waistline where she knew he had his piece stashed. She had to think of something and she had to do it fast.

"I saw all that shit you had laid out on the table and—uh…I was just wondering if I could have some," Keisha lied with a straight face.

Lloyd stared at her in silence as he sized up her facial expression to decipher whether she was telling the truth or not. Her eyebrow started twitching from nervousness and she said a silent prayer that he didn't notice.

"I haven't done nothin' in a while, but…I just need something to take the edge off. There's a lot of shit goin' on, ya know?" she continued as she absentmindedly caressed the scar on her head.

Lloyd's face remained blank and he didn't move at all as he continued to size her up. Then suddenly his face broke into a small smile.

"Actually, I got just what ya ass need," Lloyd said to her.

Her lips parted slightly as she wondered what he was up to and watched him walk off.

She didn't have to wait long to find out. She turned to follow Lloyd back to the table where the duffle bags were still sitting, wide open with what had to be over a half a million dollars' worth of drugs inside.

Lloyd picked up a knife from the counter and cut open one of the kilos of cocaine and dumped what looked like a small mountain on the table. The aroma was so loud it made her nose crinkle as she felt a lump forming in her throat while looking at it. Fear and paranoia instantly began to consume her. She'd been sober for over a month now, but it was funny how quickly the craving returned.

Her eyes locked on the powder, then at the door. She was looking for a swift exit as she felt her heart thumping away inside of her body. She know that she needed to finesse her way out of the situation.

Lloyd was ruthless and she knew he had something up his sleeve. As she stared between him and the mountain of cocaine, she felt a seismic shiver seize her body. Once again, it was fear. Fear of the man she once loved with all of her body and soul. The smile on his face was starting to look like a sinister scowl as he watched her intensely. It seemed as though in the last month that she had been gone, he had changed drastically into someone she could no longer recognize.

"C'mon," Lloyd beckoned her over with his hand.

Keisha walked uneasily over to the table and watched as Lloyd took the knife and began to make lines of cocaine. Again, she stole a glance at the door and thought about making a dash for it.

Is he going to kill me? she thought to herself.

After making five straight lines, he looked at her with black eyes and that same blank expression on his face that he'd worn earlier. Keisha's legs began to wobble, so she sat down slowly and hoped that he hadn't noticed how badly she was shaking.

Backing away from the lines, Lloyd's eyes focused in on her and she knew what he wanted. He wanted her high and, based on his conversation, she knew exactly why. His job would be easier that way.

"I don't know—uh, I mean…I've been clean for a bit and, on second thought, I don't think it would be a good look," Keisha stammered. She started backing away from the table, but Lloyd stopped her with a subtle warning. Pulling his Glock from his waist, he placed it on the table before clasping his hands together. He did it in a way that was supposed to seem casual, but Keisha knew better. She could see the subtle threat for what it was.

"C'mon, Keesh. It'll be like old times," he said.

Old times... Keisha thought as she eyed the lines on the table. Then she looked into Lloyd's cold dark eyes and she knew right then that she had no choice. She might as well get it over with, because if she didn't Lloyd was going to end it all for her anyways.

Leaning over, Keisha snorted one line with ease. She felt the burn instantly and her eyes filled with tears. She didn't know if it was because she was back in a place that she didn't want to be in with the coke, or because she was terrified.

She found herself looking up at Lloyd teary-eyed and thought just as the cocaine began to drain down the back of her throat,

Maybe I can salvage this. Maybe I'm wrong. Maybe he still has feeling for me?

Just that fast a sheen of perspiration glistened on her forehead as she willed herself to speak. To talk from her heart.

"Lloyd." Her voice wavered as she moistened her lips with a dry tongue "...whatever I have done wrong...please—"

"For starters, why were you in the car with dude when he walked into our ambush? Were you helping that nigga get at me?"

"How was I to know... is that what this is about? Are you going to kill me now?" The words escaped her mouth in a high pitch tone.

He glared at her a moment too long, then said, "No, I'm not going to kill you," he lied with a straight face. Then added, "Stop all the blubbering. I like when you get high. I might let you suck this dick. Now snort some more of that coke." He smiled sheepishly, but his eyes remained cold as he reached over and pinched her nipple so hard that it made her wince in pain.

"Ouch!" She withdrew and noticed his erection in his pants and also something else, he had another banger tucked at his waist.

"Snort the fuckin coke!" he barked, catching her off guard and causing her to flinch uncontrollably.

She was momentarily thrown off by his brass coldness, but the euphoria of the coke was really starting to kicked in. It was also making her conscious of everything around her like a 3D movie. Her paranoia increased tenfold. She could feel her heart racing and pounding in her chest even faster than it had already been.

He took another step forward and unzipped his pants. "Sniff that shit and let a nigga get some of that smokin' head."

She shifted in her seat uncomfortably, "Lloyd, why you treating me like this?"

"Like what?" he asked and crinkled his brow at her.

"Like I didn't used to be your chick… like what we had didn't mean shit... You scaring me," her voice whined.

"Truth is, what you did was dumb as fuck."

"Whaat?!" she asked in a loud screech that gave way to her fear.

"You was with that nigga. You saw too much. You saw niggas' faces and what happened and shit, Keisha. You just shouldn't have been there. This is bigger than me."

"I didn't see nothing! I don't want to have nothing to do with this and when the cops came asking, I told them that. Honest, I swear to God you gotta believe me!" Tears welled up in her eyes and intuitively she knew at that moment that she was actually begging for her life.

Lloyd rubbed his hands together causing large baguette diamonds to sparkle on his pinkie finger when he suddenly said, "The thing is, I want to believe you. I have to believe you, but this is much bigger than me...than us. I need to give it some thought. It would help if you at least tried to comfort my mind."

With that being said, he took his penis out and began to stroke it as he reached for the coke and pushed the mountain towards her.

Again, she stole a glance at the door before looking back up at him. She knew Lloyd like a book. He loved getting his dick sucked more than anything, but he especially loved how she did it for him. She would let him cum in her mouth, swallow every drop of it and savor the taste like it was sweet molasses. He seemed to like that more than anything. She did all the freaky things that Dior wouldn't do.

The problem was Keisha was no longer his lady and the last thing in the world she wanted to do was perform oral sex. But then reality set in. Her life may have been depending on it.

"I'll do whatever it takes to get back into your loving grace," she said still stalling for time as she did what she was asked.

With one hand, she grabbed his penis affectionately and, with her other hand, she leaned over and sniffed up one of the huge lines of coke he had placed in front of her. Instantly, the second blast of the potent drug was stronger than the last. She felt her mind reeling and staggering. It felt as if red, white and blue psychedelic lights exploded behind her eyes, igniting her brain. Her breathing quickened and she found herself stroking him faster and faster; the way he liked it.

"Ohhh, shit," he moaned lasciviously and began to hump her hand. Then suddenly he grabbed her by the back of her neck and forced her to her knees on the floor in front of him with his crooked dick dangling just inches from her face.

His weakness would be her strength she thought to herself. She would give him the best head of his life if that would keep her alive.

"Put it in your mouth," he said in a softer tone with lustful eyes. He licked his lips with anticipation while he looked down at her.

"You promise me you ain't going to hurt me? After it's over with, can we talk things over? I promise I'ma be loyal to you even as a side chick if that's what you want me to be."

He smacked her in the face with his penis and then tried to shove it in her mouth, nearly jabbing her in the eye. She grabbed his penis. Firm veins protruded from the bulbous mushroom head, causing Lloyd to gasp in ecstasy from the feel of her soft hand. She was playing her strength and assuaging his weakness.

"Yeah, yeah... hell yeah," he said.

He grabbed her head, palming it and forced his way into her mouth. Keisha welcomed him by opening her jaws wide and took him all the way to the back of her throat. She watched him raise up on his tiptoes like he was riding a gigantic weave. The entire time she was glancing at the door and trying to think of a way out as she deep throated him again with her mouth like a human vacuum. She slurped and sucked a dribble of pre-cum off his staff and saliva dangled from her chin.

"G… g… g… goddamn, gurl, you can suck a dick!" he stuttered as he rode the ebb and tide of her skillful mouth's manipulation.

"Oh, God," she groaned taking her mouth off him. She startedg stroking him like a plunger with one hand while wiping frantically at her nose with the other. She momentarily closed her eyes and saw white images flash on the screen of her mind. It was Lloyd placing a gun to her head. The dope had her hallucinating.

Lawd, I'm so high, she thought.

Keisha looked up at Lloyd and saw that he had his head back and eyes closed as he enjoyed the pleasure that she was giving him. With her other hand, she reached in her back pants pocket and pulled out her cellphone. Without being able to look at the screen, she tried her hardest to key in 9-1-1 from memory of where the buttons should have been on her phone. Then she slipped the phone quickly back in her pocket and prayed to God that she'd been able to do what she had been trying to do.

Keisha opened her eyes in a flash when she felt movement above, half-expecting to see Lloyd with a gun aimed at her head. He did have the gun in his hand, but he had pulled it from his waist and placed it on the table slightly out of reach from her. Then he adjusted slightly as he tried to get more comfortable. Keisha started shuttering again from fear and hoped that Lloyd hadn't seen her with her cellphone in her hand just seconds before. .

"Wha-da- fuck wrong wit'cha?!" Lloyd yelled and raised his hand like he was about to slap her.

Instead, he pushed her hand off his penis and shoved it back in her mouth all the way to her esophagus causing her to choke and gag as he forced himself down her throat and began to fuck her face in rhythmic strokes. It took everything in her power to keep her composure and to keep calm as he forced himself in her mouth. She glanced up at his maniacal face as he continued to deep stroke her mouth until he was right on the fringe of an orgasm. She could see from the scowl on his face and by the way he rammed his manhood in and out her mouth painfully down the back of her throat that this was the violent part of Lloyd that she had never wanted to see.

Then it happened. His body began to shake and shiver with his legs wobbling like he was having a seizure . He grabbed her head, causing her to gargle and gag with his dick in her mouth. The pain from his hand pressed to the side of her head with the stitches was painful. Then he came in her mouth and his violent thrashing slowed. She didn't swallow his semen. The white substance dribbled from her lips on to the floor as he pulled out of her mouth.

He frowned at her as he noticed the cum on his expensive shoes.

"What da fuck!" He took a tentative step back, looking between her and his shoes as his dick dangled in front of her. Then he let it go. Something else was on his mind.

"Bitch take them fuckin' clothes off. I wanna hit you in the ass now," he said while stroking himself wantonly.

Absentmindedly, Keisha rubbed at the sore spot on her head, checking for blood. There was none, but it still hurt.

"Lloyd, why you doing this to me?" Her voice gave way to tears causing her bottom lip to tremble. She wanted to talk some sense into him.

He reached back to hit her, but then his phone chimed on the table in front of them next to his gun and he stopped. She heard him mutter under his breath as he peered over at the caller I.D.

"Dior. What the fuck she callin' a nigga for now. Shit!"

This was the first time Keisha was happy to be interrupted by Lloyd's wife. In fact, she was overwhelmed with relief as she watched his eyes bulge with what looked like shock and dismay.

"Are you sure? How did they get in?" Lloyd asked as he ran his fingers across his short cropped hair.

As he listened to Dior's words, he slightly turned his back toward Keisha. She eyed the gun on the table only a few inches out of reach and her stomach churned in the pit of her gut with fear for what she was thinking.

"Grab the gun, shoot him! Kill him!" a voice in her head commanded.

"This is fuckin' crazy all my shit was in the house, my jewelry, fuckin' money in the safe, fuck!"

Just as Keisha built up the nerve to reach for the gun, Lloyd turned around nearly catching her. His brow raised a tight line across his face as he looked at her and continued to speak into the phone as if deep in thought. He glanced at his Presidential Rolex watch.

"Okay, I'll be there in a minute." He then disconnected the call, zipped his pants up and took out his phone again. He pecked on the phone as he muttered under his breath and began pacing the floor.

"We got a change of plans. Somebody is on their way up to keep you company. I want you to be nice to them," he said while suddenly in a hurry. He reached for the gun, stuffed it in his pants, grabbed the three bricks of cocaine off the table and then rushed over to the closet to stash them.

Keisha should have been relieved, but she wasn't. Her gut feeling was telling her that something was terribly wrong.

"Someone? Who is it? I don't want to stay here if you leaving. I'm not feeling well Lloyd. I want to go home. Please, let me go home!" she pleaded in a high pitch tone.

Lloyd turned his back on her for a second as he grabbed a Styrofoam cup, filled it with something and turned back to her. "Here, drink this. It will make you feel better," he offered. She peered inside of the cup and saw purple liquid and began to shake her head 'No".

"You drink this, or we gone have a problem. It will make you feel better. You act like you don't trust a nigga. Now drink it!" he ordered. She could see a large angry vein protruding from his forehead. but still she hesitated.

"I'm not going to ask you no fuckin' more!" He raised his voice and placed his hand near where his waist was.

Not wanting to upset him more she took the cup and glanced inside, maybe it was her imagination, or the potent coke playing tricks on her mind, but at the bottom of the cop she noticed something orange sizzling like an Alka Seltzer. She noticed something else too. Her hand was trembling badly.

"Drink it!" he yelled.

She placed the cup to her lips hands.

KNOCK! KNOCK! KNOCK!

Somebody was at the door.

Lloyd suddenly turned with his face etched in what looked like apprehension. In that instant, Keisha tossed the contents of the cup across the room. Some of the liquid landed on the beige curtains, staining them badly. Just as Lloyd turned back around, she placed the cup to her lips, turning it up. The rim of the cup had a sour taste in her mouth, like acid, and she could see some type of crusty film at the bottom of the cup. He walked over and examined the cup and then her.

A hint of a smile creased his mouth when he said with glee,

"Shawty, in a minute you ain't gone feel shit. Sorry this had to work out like this, na' mean? But you shouldn't have got with that fuck nigga, Trigga."

Instinctively Keisha played her role. She bobbed her head and pretended to act nauseated.

"I don't feel right...what did you put in that drink?" she asked with a slur as she opened and closed her eyes like she was losing consciousness.

"Something that is going to make you sleep," he said as he walked over and peeked out the peep-hold of the door.

"Sleep?" she repeated.

"Yep, eternal sleep. Like a dirt nap. Like the kind you don't wake up from. So, just close your eyes and enjoy the ride."

In that instant, her heart nearly exploded in her chest with the anxiety of death, and just when she thought things couldn't get much worse. They did.

Lloyd opened the door and Mase stepped in. He looked haggard and slovenly dressed. His clothes where disheveled. It looked like he hadn't shaved in days. Wedged between his lips was a Black and Mild cigar with a long ash burning. In his hand was a large, green duffle bag that made a loud clinking noise when he walked in and sat it down with a thump.

Keisha continued to play her role. She let her head come to rest on the table, acting as if she was unconscious but, she was secretly spying out her partially closed right eye. Instantly, she was filled with dread when she heard Mase speak as if he was winded from whatever he was carrying in the big duffle bag.

"Damn, my nigga, dat bitch knocked out cold as fuck. Whatever the fuck you give her worked good as fuck."

"It's a horse sedative called Diazeppam with enough potency to kill three people."

"Word, dats wuz up," Mase said with a grin as he reached into the duffle bag taking out the huge, heavy chain saw and a large meat clever hatchet with serrated edges that shined ominously.

"I have to bounce. Wifey just called and said somebody broke into our crib," Lloyd said preparing to leave.

"Word?" Mase droned and puffed on the cigar dropping ashes on the floor.

"Yea, you have to cut up the body and be sure not to leave no traces of blood—".

"Yo, B, I got this. This ain't my first time murking a bitch and using the body parts for fish food," Mase responded in a hyper New York accent as he puffed on the cigar, blowing smoke at Lloyd.

"You said that shit last time and fucked up killing your brotha. That's what got us in this situation in the first place to have to body this bitch."

Mase jerked his neck like he had been slapped and screwed his face up in anger.

"Nigga, fuck you mean? It was you stuck on the side of the car holding on, screamin' n' shit like a bitch for dear life while the nigga took you on a tour round the city. You was supposed to dome the nigga."

With the quickness, Lloyd pulled his banger and cocked, but didn't aim it. It took everything in his power to bridle his seething anger when he spoke through clenched teeth, slow and deliberate.

"My nigga, you got one more time to say some fuck shit like that out your mouth to me, or else it's going to be two bodies being chopped up in this bitch."

The two stood toe-to-toe. The moment had suddenly turned volatile, on the precipice of instant bloodshed.

Silence lulled.

Finally, Mase smiled, but his eyes didn't; they were as black as coals when he shrugged his shoulders, hung his head and said with what sounded like genuine sincerity,

"Yo, you right B. Let's get this money. Man, I ain't had no sleep, my fuckin' brain hurts, I'm tired. Shit, it's frustrating trying to kill your own flesh and blood brother, even if that nigga deserve that shit. It won't happened again. That's on err'thang I love." Mase extended his fist for dap. Lloyd hesitated then finally relented and the two bumped fists.

"Yea, let's get this paper. Fuck the dumb shit," Lloyd responded and tucked his banger back in his pants. He was surprised to see Mase go straight to work by pulling a large piece of plastic from the duffle bag. It was big enough to wrap two bodies in.

"I'ma cut the bitch up in this. That way the blood won't get on nothing," Mase said while looking at Keisha as if he was doing measurements in his head, but there was something else going on inside his brain.

That bitch is one of the most beautiful chicks a nigga ever seen, he thought to himself as he glanced over and noticed her round thighs and plump ass hanging off the barstool she was seated in.

"Okay, that's good. Have you heard anything from your brother?" Lloyd questioned out of the blue.

"Naw'll, but I'll go up there and see what's up after we tie up this loose end," Mase responded grim-faced.

"Okay, you let me know. Also, you keep an eye out for them homicide cops, Burns and James. They ain't no joke."

"I ran into them at the hospital and you right. They tried that 'boo game', scary tactic shit to intimidate a nigga, so I feel you. I'm on point."

With that said, Lloyd hurried out the door. He was already late.

As soon as Lloyd was gone, Mase picked up the hatchet and walked over to Keisha. He glanced down one more time as if savoring the moment, looking at her phat ass hanging over the bar stool chair. His dick got hard as wood.

Mase wasn't a handsome man like his brother Trigga and females were not falling all over themselves to get with him. In fact, it had been nearly a month since he had sex and that had been with a crack head named Bertha. Even she didn't find him attractive and charged him extra.

One thing was on his perverted mind as he reached down and caressed Keisha's firm butt while preparing to smash her in the back of the head with the claw hook part of the hatchet. He would strip her of her clothes and fuck her on the plastic canvas on the floor. There was no way in hell he was going to let all that good pussy go to waste.

FOURTEEN

Lloyd exited the apartment in a brisk pace as balmy black clouds hung from the sky like smoke billowing. A thunderstorm was threatening to erupt. At no time did he pay attention to the black Chevy Camaro parked across the street, nor its occupants inside.

Lloyd hopped in his gold Bugatti with his mind racing in a thousand different directions. Someone had broken into his home, invading the sanctuary of his prized possession, Dior and his unborn child. And not just that, they had stolen jewelry and other items.

Speeding down Peachtree Street, Lloyd did not notice the unmarked vehicle trailing him and that was a crucial mistake, especially for the well-known kingpin of the infamous E.P.G. His mind was on Dior. She had sounded stressed on the phone, but unharmed. However, it would be hell to pay if he found out who had been in his home. He reached his hand under the dashboard and hit a switch causing the stash spot under the glove compartment to release an elegant shelf that was handcrafted and custom made. The 40 caliber Glock in a velvet cloth glimmered in the limpid light. Lloyd glanced in his rearview mirror, suddenly suspicious of something, then tucked the large, chrome plated in his pants.

Being a habitual violent offender, he was facing a life sentence if he got caught with the banger, but in the streets he would face much worse if he got caught without it by one of his adversaries. So Lloyd habitually followed the street code of a gangsta's ethics and stayed strapped until death made him part from his banger.

*****

"Unit six to unit one. Be sure to keep your eye on the residence," Detective Burns spoke into the radio as him and his partner West swerved in out of traffic tailing Lloyd's gold Bugatti. The dispatcher's voice crackled with static over the radio.

"Unit one the resident in question has a patrol car stationed nearby along with one unmarked narcotic vehicle and the fugitive task force. Will you be needing additional back up?"

Just as Detective West was about to take a large bite out of a Subway foot-long, he frowned, crinkling his brow at his partner and his mouth partially opened just as they turned onto the express way 85 south.

"What the fuck do they need the fugitive task force for? This is only supposed to be a surveillance operation. Not a take down! Besides from what we heard from the microphone the Feds planted in his house, this guy's own wife and cousin are planning on whacking him and take all his money," West said.

"I know, it's like when the predator becomes the prey and his wife is like one of them ill vixen bitches in them mafia movies. I still think we should warn him about what she's up to," Burns said to his partner with a shrug as he accelerated down the highway trying to keep the tail on the speeding Bugatti.

"Fuck naw'll! That could blow the whole operation, because as soon as we tell him his first reaction would be why in the hell do we illegally have his house and car bugged!" West commented.

"Yea, I know and the whole investigation is down the drain," Burns responded somberly.

"And you and my ass would be on Buckhead, demoted and directing traffic in the hot ass sun instead of celebrating a promotion with a cushy desk job. Fuck Lloyd! I like my job too much. Let's just get this shit handled and gather enough evidence to nail his ass and his entire posse before the cousin and wife do their thing. Then everyone gets what they want!" West said and took another large bite out his sandwich.

"Okay, I'll tell them to get rid of the cars back at his condo for now," Burns sighed. Then he remembered something. "And let's not forget that guy, our other suspect at the hospital. We need to find out how he plays into all this. I feel like he was a shooter."

"Riiiiiight, okay. Did his DNA come back on anything?" West asked and placed his hand on the dashboard as his partner raced around an eighteen wheeler truck at high speed.

"So far, nothing. And our number one witness, the girl, is up in that apartment back there where Lloyd just came out of.

LEO SULLIVAN & PORSCHA STERLING

Something is fishy about that. I don't understand why they don't have that place bugged with listening devices too."

As West talked the black sky opened up and a tempestuous clap of thunder lit up the sky and rain fell hard. He took a bite from his sandwich as he leaned forward, trying to get his vision clear as he looked through the windshield of the vehicle that was being pelted with so much rain that they could barely see the car in front of them.

"Do you still see him?" West asked anxiously.

"I think so. He was only three cars ahead of us and the good thing is he can't speed too fast in this rain."

*****

Visibility was terrible because of the pouring rain when Lloyd exited the express way. The inside of his windows were starting to fog. He hit the defog button and turned on to the main street, headed for his home in the affluent neighborhood of Alpharetta, Ga. Again, he check his rearview mirror. For some reason, he felt that something was wrong and it was gnawing at him, but he couldn't put his finger on it. Again, he glanced in his review mirror as he pulled up to the gated community. He saw nothing.

Something seemed odd to him as he drove past the grandiose homes and plush landscaping. Paranoia and apprehension were a gangsta's constant companion when you're 'bout dat life'. Besides the normal shit that he went through, there was a host of other things going on. Someone had just burglarized his home and he was trying to pull off a major caper with a dude he despised. Then, the one chick other than Dior that he thought he could trust, his mean side bitch Keisha, had crossed him and he had to have her murked, even though in his heart of hearts he still had feelings for her.

FIFTEEN

Get your ass up, Keisha, and do something, Keisha screamed in her head as she heard Mase moving around beside her.

It took everything in her power to not flinch when he palmed her ass. But when he leaned over to lick her cheek and his disgusting hot garbage scented breath invaded her nostrils, her stomach lurched and she had to pray to God that she wouldn't throw up. The only thing that kept away her natural urge to puke at the fetid smell was her will to live. She had to figure out a way to get out and fast.

But how?

As if God was answering her prayers, she heard the thump of Mase dropping the weapon in his hand down onto the floor. It landed with a thud that surprised her, but he didn't seem to notice her flinch. The next sound that she heard was him unzipping his pants.

"I wonder if that tongue still wet," he whispered to himself. Keisha's voice screamed within her mind as she prayed to God that Mase wasn't going to do what she thought.

Her most horrifying nightmare was realized when Mase grabbed her firmly by the shoulders and pulled her from the barstool.

He let her go before lowering her fully to the floor and Keisha allowed herself to fall limply. With closed eyes, she tried to strain every other sense so that she could tell what was about to happen to her. She felt two of Mase's fat, smelly fingers push into the side of her neck as he checked for a pulse.

"Still alive. Perfect," he said aloud.

Keisha felt a small burst of wind and opened her eyes a tiny bit so that she could see through as Mase wiggled his way out of his hole-filled boxers. She snapped her eyes closed just as he turned around back to her. Grabbing her by her neck, Mase lifted Keisha up and pushed her head towards his groin area. Keisha held her breath to block out the sour smell coming from his body. She felt increasingly nauseated as the heat from his labored breathing hit her forehead and his coiled, rough pubic hair tickled her nose.

"I'mma see what dat mouf bout then I'mma tap up in that ass real quick. Yeah…dat's what I'mma do," Mase said growing increasingly excited with each word as he masturbated with his hands. A dribble of salvia ran down his mouth like he was fiending.

The next thing Keisha knew he was forcing her mouth open with one of his big, burly hands. The salty taste from his fingers made her eyes tear up immediately. She peeked through her eyes and saw his fat, disgusting organ bobbing in front of her face as he stroked himself faster and faster, for some reason he was grunting and making some type of noise with his throat. The first thing she noticed was what looked like black, bumpy burn marks all over the top of his penis. Keisha's stomach flipped and the taste of bile rose up in the back of her throat.

Once he got her mouth open, he wasted no time dropping his fat, thick and rotten-smelling dick inside. Keisha, no longer able to put on the charade of being drugged and unconscious, gagged and chocked as he pushed it into her mouth.

Hell to the FUCK no! she thought to herself. And with that, she clamped her teeth together. Right on Mase's rock hard rod.

"AHHHHHHHHH SHHIIIIIIIIITTTTTT!" Mase yelled out loud. He tried to pull away from Kiesha's jaws, but the only thing that did was cause him more pain as she continued to clamp down on his flesh. She felt the salty taste of blood mix with the sour taste of his flesh in her mouth. It repulsed her, but in her crazed state, she couldn't force her jaws to let go.

"PLLLLEAAAAASEEEE, OHHH GAAAAWWWWWDDD!!!" Mase yelled out for mercy as she continued to clamp down. It wasn't until he dropped to his knees that she finally released him. Opening her eyes, she wiped the blood from her mouth and spit out as much as she could as she watched him writhing on the floor, holding his nearly severed member in his hands as he yelped out in pain and anguish.

"Pleeeease, Pleeeease …." he wailed like a wounded animal as he held on to his penis. Petrified, Keisha took a timid step back prepared to run and leave. Then was the time to make her escape if any. Just as she stepped over him, he grabbed her leg in what felt like a vice grip and yanked her back with so much force her neck snapped back and she nearly fell.

"Bitch I'mma kill your ass!" Mase exclaimed was crying real tears through blood shot red colored eyes.

He yanked her foot again as she tried to get away, causing her right knee to buckle. She fell right on top of him, landing in his lap. Just as he reached back to punch her in her face, she ducked and the blow connected with the side of her head. She just happened to see a porcelain lamp on the table that was shaped like an exotic teardrop. She grabbed it and crashed it upside his head, causing fragments to shatter. A lone piece of the porcelain cut into her hand and she held on to it like a knife. She was prepared to gouge his eyes out with it as a trickle of blood ran down his forehead. To her utter disbelief, like a giant his large head toppled backwards and hit the floor with a thump. He was knocked out cold and his body started convulsing violently as if he was having a seizure as he made gurgling noises with his mouth.

Keisha's eyes widened as she looked at the sight before her. It was almost as if she snapped out of whatever zone she'd been in and now she was seeing the horror of what she'd done. Running into the master bedroom, she changed quickly out of her own clothes, grabbed a pair of jean shorts and threw a tank top over her head. She jogged to the bathroom and rinsed her mouth out quickly then gargled once with mouthwash. After looking at herself in the mirror to make sure that she didn't look suspicious, or anything like how she felt, she ran to the closet where Lloyd kept his money.

Looking in the closet, she took a deep breath before grabbing over ten bands of hundred dollar bills and stuffed them in a small brown tote that was next to the bed. She was about to close the closet when suddenly her eyes locked on a few small baggies of coke. After fighting a mental battle with herself, she grabbed five bags, stuffed them in the tote and closed the closet door.

Keisha ran out of the bedroom door and didn't slow down not even when she passed an unconscious Mase on the floor, still bleeding profusely from his groin area. Snatching the door open, she was greeted by the sound of thunder and lightning as an onslaught of rain fell down upon her head. Keisha didn't care about the rain because she could see something else off in the distance that caught her attention and made her heart lurch in her chest.

Taking off in a brisk walk and then a jog, she ran off in the direction of what she saw. There was a person…a male, laid out on the wet, green grass near a man-made pond at the entrance of the condo subdivision. He was wearing a white hospital gown that had red spots of what looked to be blood decorating the chest area.

As soon as Keisha reached him, she dropped to her knees and grabbed his head in her hands.

"Trigga! Oh my God! What are you doin' here?" she yelled as she searched his face to see any trace of life. She felt tears stinging her eyes even though she didn't quite know why. Although she didn't really know Trigga all that much, the small amount of time they had known each other had been filled with so many high intensity moments, that she couldn't help but feel connected to him in some way.

"Your phone…you messaged me…" he said slowly, then twisted up his face in pain.

"My phone?" Keisha asked with a confused look as the rain beat down on both of their faces.

"Yeah, you…"

"I gotta get you out this fuckin' rain," Keisha said suddenly as the rain started falling harder. Then she thought about Lloyd. If he returned and saw both of them sitting right in front of the entrance to his condo they would both be dead.

Grabbing her phone from her pocket, she unlocked it so that she could call Uber to pick them up. Her eyes fell upon the last thing she'd done with her phone. It was a text message to Trigga's phone that shared her GPS location.

So that's how he found me, she thought to herself as she clicked off the screen.

She had been trying to dial 9-1-1, but ended up shooting her location over to Trigga instead. He'd been the last person who had called her phone back at the hospital so the screen had been set on his phone number. Once again, fate had brought them together.

She covered Trigga as best as she could and cradled him in her arms as she waited for the vehicle to arrive and take them away from Lloyd's place. She looked down at him and noticed that he was looking directly into her eyes, but in his eyes was a distant look, as if he wasn't completely there.

"I have to get you to the hospital," Keisha said through tear-filled eyes. She looked at the blood on the front of the gown. It wasn't much, but there was no telling what injuries were underneath.

"No," he said. "I know someone. Just…take me home."

"Home?" Keisha said furrowing her eyebrows. "To New York?"

"No," Trigga said. Then he screwed his face up and tried with great effort to lift up from her arms.

"No, please! I don't think you should—"

Trigga ignored her as he still struggled to get to his feet. Kiesha jumped up, fully aware that he was not going to listen to her and decided to help him up instead. Grabbing one of his arms, she pulled it over her shoulders and held him firmly with her other arm as he fell into her for support.

"You okay?" Keisha asked him as she wiped away the rain from her face with one hand.

Trigga nodded, although his face was still twisted. He grabbed at his chest, right above the spot of blood on his gown. Then suddenly he began to smile with a twinkle in his eyes and Keisha frowned up at him.

Oh, God. He must be going into shock, she thought to herself.

"Look, a nigga lookin' bad right now and all, but I need you to promise me one thing," he said with a smirk lightly.

"What?" Keisha asked as she shifted her feet to support his weight.

"Can you check to see if a nigga ass is out in this fuckin'
gown? Ain't a good look for a nigga to be walkin' around bleeding
and shit through his chest and his ass out," Trigga said with a
strained smile. It was obvious that he was in a considerable amount
of pain, but his gangsta pride wouldn't allow him to be shameful.

Keisha shot him a blank look then. Despite their grim
situations, she couldn't help but smile back at him in the pouring
rain. For some strange reason, she felt a connection like gravity was
pulling her soul into him as her nurturing instincts kicked in. After
everything that she'd been through the last couple weeks—hell, the
last *month,* she didn't think she'd ever smile again. It felt good to
finally be able to find something humorous for a minute after
spending so much time fighting for her life. Trigga must have felt
the same way because he continued to radiate in an amber glow that
had her resisting the urge to kiss his luscious lips shimmering in the
rain.

"You're all good. I promise I'll help you cover your ass,
Trigga," Keisha said as she wiped the rain from his face
affectionately and gave her surrounding a quick once over. They
needed to get moving just in case Mase came running out the house
holding his nearly severed penis in one hand and a gun that had a
bullet with her name on it in the other.

"Any chick that helps a nigga cover his ass is good with me,"
Trigga joked, but Keisha caught his play on words. He was thanking
her in the literal sense for helping to keep him from having his

natural ass exposed in his hospital gown, but he was also giving her a cryptic thank you for not snitching on him to the cops.

Keisha just looked at him and nodded her head as he looked into her eyes. They didn't say a word to each other then, but they didn't need to. Neither one of them knew why the last few events that had brought them together had occurred, but they knew one thing. They were both happy that it did.

SIXTEEN

Lloyd walked into his home mad as hell at what he saw. Everything was trashed. His expensive furniture was ripped up and everything inside had been pulled out. It looked like the Feds had ransacked his place rather than some niggas on an opposing team. They had searched everything in the house trying to find either his money stash, or his dope.

"I can't take this shit anymore Lloyd! I want out! What if I had been here? What if our daughter had been born and she was in here?" Dior screeched to the top of her lungs at Lloyd as she cried and wiped tears from her face.

Lloyd bit his lip and glared around the house as he listened to her scream. She had a valid point, because he'd thought of the same thing. What he couldn't understand though was how someone had gotten through his top-notch security system. It was burglarproof...state of the art. There was nothing like it and to think that some small-time Atlanta dope boys might have been able to run right in his shit didn't sit right with him. His spot was locked down like Fort Knox. There was no breaking in.

"How the hell they get in?" Lloyd asked Dior suddenly.

"What you mean?" she asked him. She gestured at the broken glass at the back door. "They broke in through the back." Her crying came to a sudden halt and the tears that had been on her face seconds ago dried up. Lloyd noticed it immediately, but played it cool.

"Through the back, huh?" Lloyd said as he crooked his neck to the side and looked at Dior.

"Yeah…I mean, how else would they have gotten in?" she asked as she looked at him. A faint hint of panic and alarm lingered in her eyes. It wouldn't have been noticeable to the normal eye, but Lloyd knew his wife and he could tell when she was about that bullshit.

"C'mere, Dior. I think I know how we can figure out who did this," Lloyd said. He grabbed her by her arm and half-dragged her to his office down the hall from them.

"What you mean? I—I—how are we gonna…"

"Sit down," Lloyd said as he pushed her down on the large leather chair inside of his office. It was the chair reserved for him and him alone, but in this case, he wanted Dior to sit in it because it was the best seat to get a good look at what she was about to see.

"Okay," Lloyd said as he grabbed a remote from off the desk.

Sitting on the desk in front of Dior, he clicked a button on the remote and TV monitors descended from above. Once they were settled, Lloyd hit another button that made the screens come on and when Dior saw what was on them, she nearly fainted.

"So these are the monitors that show the perimeter of our home," Lloyd said. "And if I hit this button," Lloyd tapped a button. "...I can rewind the cameras that I have installed around the perimeter and it will show me exactly what happened.

Dior felt herself almost about to hyperventilate as Lloyd started to rewind the tapes.

"I thought we only had the camera at the front..." Dior said quietly as she watched. She felt tears come to her eyes. She prayed inside that God would intervene and stop what was about to happen from happening.

"I know you did," Lloyd said as he turned and winked at her with his black eyes that were so hollow and dead at the moment it was like looking into a black hole. "I got these installed recently, but I haven't had time to check them because I've been tending to other shit."

Lloyd continued to rewind and then he stopped suddenly when something caught his eye. Dior felt herself grow weak and grabbed at her belly.

"Well, look at dis shit," Lloyd said quietly as he looked at the screen.

On the screen was Kenyon and Dior in a tight embrace as they shared a passionate kiss. It was right after they had set what they believed was the scheme of the year. They'd staged everything at the home as a robbery and stolen all of Lloyd's money out of the main vault on the lower level of the home.

The plan was that Kenyon would run away with the money and Dior would claim that she no longer wanted to be with Lloyd for fear of her and their child's safety. She would check in at a hotel like she normally did when she threatened to leave Lloyd and he would give her the customary three days of no contact that he always did before he found her and tried to win her back. The difference was, this time when he went to find her, it would have been too late. She and Kenyon would have been sipping Pina Coladas in the Bahamas by then on his dime and he would never be able to find either of them.

One thing they forgot about was that Lloyd was the most paranoid nigga in the universe and, although most times it was in vain, this time his paranoia had spoiled their plans.

"It's—it's not what you think!" Dior yelled out in horror as Lloyd turned to look at her. The look in his eyes was one that she'd never seen before directed at her. Lloyd had always looked at her with love, care and affection, even when they were going through shit.

"Yeah, okay," Lloyd said quietly. He got up and walked out of the office, leaving Dior with her racing thoughts.

She had no idea what Lloyd was up to, but she knew that there was no way he would give up that easily. By the end of the night, if she didn't find a way to get out or get help, she would be dead. Jumping up, she reached for the phone sitting on top of Lloyd's large, mahogany executive desk. Just as she grabbed it, she heard a gun cock from behind her.

"Put that muthafucka down now before I blow yo' bird ass brains out, you dumb bitch," Lloyd's voice said from behind her. Dior froze in place…all except for her chest that was heaving up and down from her short, powerful breaths.

I'm gonna die, Dior thought to herself. As if hearing her thoughts, Lloyd responded.

"I'm not gonna kill you," he said. Dior felt herself relax a small bit. "Not yet anyways. Not while you got my seed in you. So…I gotta get her out."

After Lloyd's words registered in Dior's brain, she jerked around to face him, fear once again clenched her body so tightly that she felt like she couldn't breathe. She felt herself swoon a little as the thought of what Lloyd meant crossed her mind.

*****

Burns looked at his partner as they listened to the audio together.

"Should we go in?" he asked West.

West had his lips pulled into a straight line as he thought about what they should do. If someone was going to be killed, they couldn't just sit there and let it happen. Even if the wife had planned on possibly killing her husband anyways.

"Let's wait a minute. He didn't say for a fact that he would kill her yet. And from what I've heard so far, there is no money and no dope in the house. If we run in there now, we ain't got shit to pin on him at all! Not even a possession charge!"

Burns nodded his head. His partner was right. They should wait until something happened that would stick to Lloyd. They had been trying to catch that asshole for a while now and he didn't want all of the work he'd done to go to shit. He'd spent too many nights away from his wife and kids to let it all be washed away for acting too fast. He'd waited years. He could wait a little longer.

"Okay, we wait, but if he tries to kill her, we gotta go," Burns said. West nodded.

*****

"Oh, my God," Dior whispered as she looked at Lloyd. "You're goin' to cut my baby out!" She clasped her hands around her stomach and opened her mouth to let out a long, heart-wrenching wail.

"Shut that noisy shit up!" Lloyd said as he backhanded her. She fell backwards, stumbled over the leg of his desk chair and then landed on the floor, right on her ass, with a loud thump. Within seconds, Lloyd was on her like a silver back gorilla beating her in the face with his fists.

"You need to be more muthafuckin' careful that you don't hurt my gotdamn seed!" Lloyd warned her once he was done pummeling her face to a pulp.

Dior looked up at him, in half a daze. Her vision was blurred from his attacks and her body was weak. She felt a sharp pain shooting through her belly, but she couldn't even lift a finger to hold it. Her breathing slowed and she let her head hang to the side as Lloyd towered above her.

"I'mma tie you up. You ain't gone leave the fuckin' bed until I have someone come down here to make you deliver my seed. But before you do that, you need to call that nigga Kenyon and tell him to come here. I'mma murk his ass right in front of you so you can have the pleasure of watchin' the show," Lloyd said with a sinister smile on his dark, black face as he divulged his plan.

"Please, just let me go," Dior pled.

"I'mma let you go," Lloyd said. "But it's gonna be in a fuckin' body bag. Get your ass up!"

Without waiting for Dior to try to move, Lloyd reached down, grabbed her hair and then wound it around his fist. He used it to bring her to her feet, nearly pulling strands from her scalp. Dior winced from the pain and bit her lip. She didn't want to give him the satisfaction that came with crying out. One thing she knew about Lloyd was that he loved it when his victims cried and pleaded with him. To him, it was like getting a good nut when someone begged for their life, or screamed because of the pain he caused them.

Lloyd walked Dior down the hall to a room tucked at the back of the house. It was set off to the side, so it was the room that Lloyd and Dior had reserved in case her parents had ever come to visit. The thing was, they couldn't stand Lloyd and had nearly disowned Dior for marrying him, so they never came. The room was the perfect place to stash Dior. It was so far from everything that he wouldn't have to hear her cries.

As Lloyd prepared to tie Dior down he heard his phone ringing, but he ignored it. He had other things to tend to at the moment; a more pressing matter. Whoever was on the phone just had to either call back later or leave a message.

Whap!

Lloyd smacked Dior hard across the face as he grabbed her arm to tie it up to the bedpost.

"Shut up that damn whimpering! You wasn't fuckin' cryin' when you had that nigga up in here was stealing all my shit!" Lloyd yelled out and some particles of his spit fell on her face with his words. "How many time he get the pussy, huh? You let that nigga fuck you in here? You suck his dick and kissing me?"

Dior's eyes opened wide although they were starting to swell as she looked at Lloyd and prayed he didn't really expect an answer. He bared his teeth and looked at her as she watched him in silence.

"I asked you a fuckin' question!" he roared. "DID YOU FUCK HIM IN MY SHIT?!"

"NO! NO! Dior cried out with her vision blared, she was seeing stars as she lied, but she hoped to hell that Lloyd believed it.

"You—are—a—got—damn—LIAR!" Lloyd yelled like a craved manic and punched her over and over again in her face and neck as he spoke. Suddenly his phone began ringing again.

"SHIT!" he yelled out. Looking at Dior in a rage, his fists were bloody. He noticed that she seemed to be nearly unconscious from the beating he'd given her and one arm was securely tied at the wrist to the bed post. She wouldn't be going anywhere soon.

Lloyd turned to leave the room and walked back to his office to grab his phone.

"WHAT?!" Lloyd yelled into the phone once he saw who had been blowing up his phone.

"ARRRRRGGGGHHHHHHHH, that biiiiiiiitch!" Mase yelled out in his ears. Lloyd pulled the phone away from him and glared at it.

"Man, why the fuck you hollerin' like a bitch? The hell wrong wit' yo' ass?"

"Sh—she—she…that bitch—she got me!"

Lloyd could feel his blood boiling as he listened to Mase stutter through the phone. He still didn't know what the fuck he was sputtering about, but he did know one thing. Mase had fucked up and it would be his last fuck up of his life.

I'mma dead this nigga on sight ASAP! Tonight, Lloyd thought to himself.

"Is she there?" Lloyd asked him as he absent-mindedly watched Dior writhing in pain. He assumed that some way Keisha wasn't dead yet, and although that perplexed him, he needed to know how bad the situation was over there with Mase before he tried to figure out why his sedative didn't work.

"No! She—"

Lloyd hung up before Mase was even able to finish up his sentence.

"FUCK!" he yelled out. "I *knew* better! FUUUUUUCK!"

Lloyd punched the wall in his office five times in a row, making five neat holes in the wall. Still, his anger was at an all-time high. He couldn't figure out who he should get to first, Kenyon or Mase.

Grabbing his keys, Lloyd put Trigga to the back of his mind and focused on his two new targets, Mase and Kenyon.

As soon as Lloyd walked out to his car, he was hit with a pleasant surprise. Kenyon's blue Aston Martin pulled up curbside. Lloyd wiped a hand over his face and tried to relax as he saw his cousin hop out of his ride with a worried look on his face.

"What's goin' on, nigga?" Lloyd asked him as he leaned against his Bugatti.

The rain had finally stopped, the sun was sitting high in the sky and beaming down on his face. The light caused his black skin to glow, but not in a way that seemed heavenly. It was an evil glow that matched the forced grin on his face. Lloyd was trying to appear calm, but his face twitched uncontrollably as he resisted the urge to pull out his banger, shoot Kenyon in the head at point blank range and murder his cousin, his own blood, in broad daylight. Instead a slight growl escaped his mouth as he pictured his cousin in his home dicking down his wife.

Kenyon, however, was too distracted to notice. He'd been calling Dior's phone since he'd left earlier, but she hadn't answered once; not even his texts. He wasn't sure what was going on with her, but his fear was that Lloyd had convinced her once again to stay and she was having second thoughts. He couldn't have been further from the truth.

"Aye, nigga," Kenyon greeted Lloyd with his eyes focused on the house in front of him. "Dior told me some niggas hit yo' spot up. Everything a'ight? She in there?"

Lloyd sneered at Kenyon with pure hatred with his jaw clenched so tight his teeth gritted loudly.

Blow his fuckin' brains out. Push his wig back! a voice demanded in the back of his
mind.

Suddenly Lloyd began to shake like his body was going into a convulsive trimmer. He was fuming mad and with one quick motion he reached for his banger and simultaneously grabbed Kenyon by his collar, shoving the barrel of the pistol in his mouth with so much force that he broke several front teeth. The deadly assault caused Kenyon to cry out in excruciating pain and terror.

"Fuck nigga, you been in there fuckin' my wife and you suppose'ta be my own cousin, my own flesh and fuckin' blood!!" Lloyd cocked the gun. The metallic sound resonated.

Instantly, Kenyon knew his life was a wrap in the foggy haze of being dazed from the blow of the gun's impact. His mind went into survival mode as he teetered on the balls of his feet and then on his toes. With the large barrel of the gun in his mouth, he managed to let out a bloodcurdling scream.

"Man nooooo, pleasssssss!!" he screamed so loud his voice echoed like they were in the Grand Canyon causing the birds to take flight from the sanctuary of the tries to flock to safety high in the sky.

*****

West gasped at what he was seeing ahead of him. The situation had escalated fast.

"Is he about to kill him in broad day—?"

"WEST! Move your ass!" Burns yelled as he snatched at the handle of his door. After forcing it open so hard that he probably almost broke the handle, Burns jumped out, grabbed his gun from his side and then took off running down the street towards where Kenyon and Lloyd stood.

"I'm coming! SHIT!" West said. He jumped out and ran behind Burns towards the two men, half-thinking about how much he wished that they had more to pin on Lloyd than a simple attempted murder charge. He wanted Lloyd to go down for the rest of his natural life without any room to wiggle. This wasn't how all of his work on the case was supposed to go down.

*****

"Nigga, we slept on the same pissy ass mattress. I looked out for you, fought battles for you. Now you do this fuck shit. It's over, nigga. My auntie's gonna dress your punk ass up in a black suit that I'll have the honor of buying for you!" Lloyd gritted through his teeth. He was a hairpin away from pulling the trigger.

Kenyon continued to frantically babble and pleaded for his life with the gun in his mouth, ready and cocked to send him to his maker. His worst fear had been realized. Lloyd now knew what had been going on behind his back and he'd killed Dior and the baby. Kenyon hadn't been able to protect the one person on Earth he loved more than himself. If Lloyd didn't kill him, he made up his mind that he'd kill himself.

"Any last words, pussy nigga?!" Lloyd yelled in his face.

The way Lloyd's insane eyes looked with his finger inches away from pulling the trigger, Kenyon knew that his worst fear had come true. Pussy over loyalty had caused a many a nigga an untimely demise and so was the case with Kenyon. He'd experienced Dior's love, but he didn't know that the need for love was greater than loyalty. Love could turn even the most loyal nigga into the most disloyal. You did things for the people you loved that you would later hate yourself for—all because you wanted them to be loved back.

Dior had done it for Lloyd and I did it for her, he thought as the barrel of the gun was shoved so deep in his mouth that it nearly touched his tonsils.

With blood red eyes, hands shaking, pulse racing with full intent on squeezing the trigger, Lloyd couldn't help but say his last words menacingly as if to redeem what was stolen; the virtuosity of his prized possession being his woman.

His hand tightened to pull the trigger...

"FREEZE! Drop your weapons!" Detective Burns yelled as he ran seemingly out of nowhere, catching Lloyd by surprise . He'd been so preoccupied and focused on offing Kenyon that he hadn't even realized that they had company until it was too late.

Detective West ran up next, winded, tired and breathing hard like a two pack a day smoker. He was out of breath as he stood next to his partner and seconds after Burns already had his weapon pulled and trained on Lloyd's skull. He seriously needed to get in shape and he made a mental note to focus on that as soon as he was able to make it out of this situation.

He raised his weapon as well and focused it on Lloyd, the notorious gangster he had been hunting down for most of his career. Years ago, nothing would have pleased him more than to put a bullet right in the fucker's face, but he had told himself back then that there would be much more pleasure gained from being able to stick him with a fat load of evidence, so he could sit behind bars with every enemy he had shitted on to get to the top. Lloyd wouldn't last three months in lock up before someone killed him. He had so many enemies waiting for him that his chance of survival was minimal and they would all bond together over a common enemy.

"DROP YOUR WEAPON!" Burns yelled out again beside him.

West waited as he watched Lloyd turn from them back to his cousin standing in front of him as blood oozed from Kenyon's mouth. Both cops could tell that Kenyon was undeniably happy to see them.

Then something insane happened. Something that West wouldn't have expected even from a crazy lunatic like Lloyd. Lloyd continued to shove the gun down his throat, finger on the trigger, determined to get rid of his cousin whether they had their guns aimed at him, or not.

With horror etched across his chubby face, West turned towards his partner because he knew exactly how this was about to go down and it wasn't how he wanted it. Burns was going to kill Lloyd and with him everything that West had wanted would die. West's chances of catching the most notorious kingpin in Atlanta who had terrorized so many would be gone. The promotion that he'd been promised, the corner office, the fat raise…all of it would be gone.

"NOOOOOO!" West yelled out. He batted Burns' hand down just as he fired his weapon. But it was too late. The bullet fired out of the chamber and lodged right into Lloyd before he could discharge his own weapon. The force of the bullet ripped his own gun out of his hand and it landed a few feet from him. Then he fell, dropping to his knees. His face was still laced with all of the hate he felt as he continued to stare at his cousin.

Lloyd clutched his side where the bullet had pierced him in agonizing pain.

West's heart nearly leaped out of his chest. Maybe Lloyd could be saved!

"West! What the fuck is wrong with you?!" Burns yelled at him as he grabbed his phone to call for an ambulance.

"Nothing. Grab the cousin and put him in the back of the car so we can question him. He may be inclined to share some evidence with us…enough for us to put away this bastard for good," West said as he pulled the phone to his ear.

He looked at the scene ahead of him. Lloyd was still on his knees with his jaw clenched tight and a seething look of anger on his face. Kenyon had taken the opportunity to run pass him and into Lloyd's home, most likely to check on the wife. West smiled to himself as he rattled off the instructions to dispatch for the ambulance. It was a good thing they had sat back while Lloyd beat the shit out of his own wife. It might be just what they needed to convince Kenyon to rat out his cousin. Women have brought down empires. Surely, one could turn one street thug against another, even if they were blood.

SEVENTEEN

One Month Later

"Still thinkin' about him, huh?" Tish asked Keisha as she looked at her friend who was staring off into space.

Keisha turned her attention towards Tish and grinned, exposing the truth before she even had the chance to speak it.

"Yeah, I mean...I just wonder if I'll ever see him again. He texts me from time to time to see if I'm okay, but beyond that...nothing," Keisha thought sadly as she thumbed through her messages.

The day she found Trigga laying in the grass in front of Lloyd's condo about a month back was the last time she'd seen him, but she thought about him every single day. She helped him back to his hotel room that day and he had called someone he knew to come over and tend to his wombs. Whoever it was definitely wasn't a physician...not any physician Keisha knew, but he definitely knew his stuff.

Within hours, Trigga was patched up and recovering well. He told her that she could sleep in the second room in his suite and she happily obliged. When she woke up in the morning, he was gone. He sent her a text to her phone saying that he had gone back to New York and she would be safe because Lloyd was in prison. He told her to let him know if she needed anything and, besides the occasional text to check on her well-being, that was that.

He'd also left her with some cash as 'an apology' for getting her fired from her job. Keisha was still stressing because she knew she had to cover the rest of her tuition in order to start classes, but she received a call the next day that her balance was paid and she could start school that Fall. Part of her wondered if Trigga had paid that too, but there was no way he would have known about her attending Clark Atlanta that Fall so she shook off the thought and thanked God for her blessing.

When she called Tish to thank her for visiting her at the hospital she found out that Tish was going through her own struggles. She'd lost her apartment and needed a place to stay. It was the perfect situation because Keisha could use a roommate to help her cover part of the rent.

"I think the whole thing is kind of surreal, ya know?" Tish said as she smacked her gum loudly and fell onto the bed next to where Keisha sat. "I mean, it's like the typical boy meets girl story with a hood, gangsta twist. What the fuck kinda shit is that?" Tish laughed.

"I don't know, but it's crazy. When I met him at the club it felt like I already knew him. That's the only reason I felt comfortable enough to ask him for a ride. Then all that crazy shit happened after…I still can't believe Lloyd is in prison. Well, jail…since he hasn't gone to trial yet, I should say."

"What do you think happened to the guy who tried to kill you? Lloyd's friend?" Tish asked. Keisha turned and looked her right in her eyes, but it was almost like she was looking through them as she thought back to the gruesome event when she'd nearly severed Mase's penis with her teeth. She omitted that part of the story when she filled Tish in on the past events concerning Trigga and Lloyd.

"Um, I don't know. But Lloyd is the leader so without him, his niggas ain't shit," Keisha told herself more than Tish. She wanted to believe the words to be true because if she felt like Mase was still after her, she wouldn't be able to sleep at night, or even walk outside her front door.

"Well, I ain't no goon or nuthin', but I can wield a bat around like a damn Kung Fu killer, so we good up in here!" Tish joked as she ran her fingers through her long hair. Looking at Tish made her miss her own long tresses. Her hair was starting to grow back over the bald spot she'd had from where the stitches were placed, but it had grown in at odd angles and didn't lay just right.

"Well, I'mma schedule an appointment to get some weave put in so I can run my fingers through my shit like you. Making me jealous and shit. I don't appreciate that," Keisha laughed.

"Yo' shit won't ever lay like mine. I got that good hair," Tish joked as she whipped her hair from side to side.

"Well, I can get that good hair, too. Right from the Beauty Mart down the way!"

Tish grabbed one of Keisha's pillows off her bed and jabbed her in the face with it. Keisha tried to duck, but it caught her in the head anyways.

"BITCH!" Keisha yelled as she laughed.

Things felt right at that moment, but in the back of her mind, Keisha wondered how long it would last.

Trigga sat across from Keisha's apartment and watched the silhouette of her tossing her hair back and laughing through her sheer yellow curtains. After a month at home, he was in Atlanta again and ready to get back on the job. His health was perfect and he was fully recovered. He hadn't seen his brother in about a month, which wasn't anything abnormal. After getting some money Mase always got lost until he was dead broke again. Then as soon as the funds ran out he was back blowing up Trigga's phone asking when the next job would be set up.

Word on the street was that Lloyd was about to be released. Somehow the gun, the main piece of evidence needed to prove the prosecution's case, had gone missing. They had been trying their hardest the last four weeks to delay as much as they could in order to keep Lloyd in jail, but they were going to have to release him. When they did, Trigga was going to be the first person waiting in line to tag that ass with one straight to the dome. There wasn't a thing he wanted more than to finally get this hit over with and move on about his business.

But for some odd reason, instead of plotting how he was going to get at Lloyd as soon as his feet hit the streets, he was in front of Keisha's apartment watching her. His mind had told him not to text her and he failed at that. He texted her every other day. Two days were about as long as he'd been able to shrug her off before he had to check in to make sure she was okay. Then he told himself not to go see her, but here he was with his ass right in front of her damn apartment. How he could be pussy whipped when he hadn't even got the pussy was beyond him.

Sighing, Trigga started his engine and placed his car in reverse. He backed out a few inches and then smashed his foot against the brakes. Then he backed out a little more, but smashed the brakes one more time. Frowning, he picked up his cellphone and looked at it.

Should I call her? he thought to himself.

Beep! Beeeeeeeeeep!

"Aye, are you movin' or what? I'm tryin' to get a park! Gotdammit!" a female voice yelled out.

Disgusted at the woman's attitude, Trigga threw his phone to the floor of the car and mashed the gas, tearing his car out of the parking spot so fast that he was only inches away from smashing into the irate woman's vehicle. He looked in his side mirror as her white face grew pale, her eyes widened and her mouth dropped open as she braced herself for the collision that never happened.

With a light chuckle, Trigga drove off in the opposite direction, speeding out of the complex and onto the main street ahead of him. He didn't even know that Keisha, who had been struck with curiosity from the noise outside of her window, was watching his exit the whole time with a confused expression on her face.

EIGHTEEN

"Mommy, please don't hurt me! I'll be a good boy, please! I promise I'll be good!" an eight year old Mase cried out as his mother tightened her grip around his wrist. He tugged back, but his little body and small strength was no match for the woman.

"Close your fuckin' mouth before I pull out your damn tongue," she barked at him.

With tears in his eyes, Mase clamped his mouth shut, but still continued to try to pull his arm from her grasp.

"Why can't you be more like Maurice? I'm tired of havin' to come up to that school because them white folks are complainin' about your dumb ass! Pull down your pants!"

Mase could no longer hold it in as the terror gripped him. Opening his mouth, he let out a wail that could chill the bone. It was the cry of a child begging for help from anyone who could hear his pleas.

But as usual, no help came.

Mase's mother ripped his pants off his body when she became unsatisfied at the speed in which he had been taking them off *himself and she grabbed his wrist and drew him closer. Her eyes were pulled into slits and her lips were formed into a tight sneer. With a horrified expression on his face that perfectly illustrated the compilation of emotions he had inside, he looked from his mother to the stove where she had a seething hot cast-iron rod lying on the largest eye. The rod was so hot that it was glowing red from the heat.*

"Please, mommy! I'm sorry, I tried my hardest, but I don't know why—I'm sorry!"

"SHUT UP!" she yelled. "These white folks want me to spend my money to put you in classes! Talking about you got dyslexia or some shit. I don't have no money for that bullshit! Yo' dumb ass already eat me out of house and home as it is! So you know what? I'mma give you somethin' to make you remember what the fuck you need to do. Every time you fuck up, this is what you get. This is what you get until you learn how to be more like Maurice!"

With that, Mase's mother grabbed the iron rod off the stove and pressed it against Mase's tiny penis. He opened up his mouth and screamed to the top of his lungs as the smell of smoldering flesh spread throughout the room. Seconds later, which really had felt like an eternity, Mase's mother removed the iron rod from his penis and watched with a cruel smile as her son dropped to his knees while holding his damaged flesh and whimpered until his voice became so hoarse he could no longer get out a word.

"Take your ass to bed early," she told Mase. "Your brother will be home from basketball practice soon. You better not mess with him and you better not tell him shit, or I'll give you some more!"

Mase did as he was told to the best of his ability, only deviating from her order once to jog wide-legged to the kitchen and grab some ice from the freezer. With the ice tightly pressed against his injury, he laid in the bed and cried himself to sleep.

Hours later he was awakened by the sound of someone in the room. When he opened his eyes, he saw his twin brother Maurice walking in with a cheerful smile on his face as he pulled off his jersey.

"Mase, man, you shoulda been there so you coulda seen that shit I did tonight! Coach said I'm the best player on the team and don't nobody got handles like me!" Maurice imitated dribbling a ball and passing it back and forth between his legs before going up for a mock lay-up.

Mase frowned up his face at his brother. "Man, shut up. I don't wanna hear that shit," he grumbled and turned to face the wall.

Maurice shrugged and continued undressing.

"Maurice!" Mase heard his mother yell out. "Did you have a good game?"

"Yeah!" Maurice exclaimed, excited to have the audience that he'd wanted. "Coach said I'm the best player on the team!"

"Really! Well, let's go celebrate. I'mma get the keys and we can drive down to the Dairy Queen," she said.

"That's what's up, ma," Maurice responded. "Mase, you wanna go?"

"No, Mase can't go. He isn't feelin' well, so he gotta stay here. Let's go, Maurice. You can order whatever you want," she said.

Maurice took another look at his brother and then shrugged. He had wanted to ask what was up with Mase, but he figured now wasn't a good time. He seemed to be in a mood or something. So instead, he grabbed a shirt, tossed it over his back and then left without speaking. Mase gritted his teeth once he heard the front door close behind them.

And the hate he would have in his heart for his brother was born.

Waking up, Mase shook off the nightmare that he'd had about his mother and ran to the bathroom to toss water on his face. Ever since that bitch, Keisha, had nearly made him an eunuch, he'd been dreaming up memories that he'd tried his hardest to forget.

He'd never gotten over how Trigga had turned the first woman he loved, his mother, against him. Ever since then, the hate he had in his heart for his brother grew and festered, but for the most part he'd been able to keep it at bay because he knew that without Trigga, he didn't have the means to survive. With their contracts, Trigga was the brains and the brawn and he merely carried Mase along for the ride. Mase was his back up, but Trigga really could pull the jobs on his own if he wanted. But Trigga never left his brother out. His heart was too big for that. He always wanted to share.

How angelic of him. How patriotic. How nice. Sweet baby Trigga, always lookin' out for the underdog, Mase thought as he glared at himself in the mirror.

Tables turned when Mase found himself falling for the first woman he'd ever loved other than his mother, Queen. Of course Queen was heavily protected, so he'd had to love her from afar, but that didn't make his love no lesser than anyone's. Every night he dreamt about her. It was to the point that he could almost feel her in his dreams. He could smell the fragrance in her long, black, curly hair. At night he would curl up in his bed and imagine that her buttery skin was rubbing against his as they succumbed to their desires and finally made love to one another.

But Trigga had stolen Queen from him too.

When she'd first hired them to kill one of her men who betrayed her, she hired both of them. Every job after, she hired both of them. She got close to both of them. She met with both of them. She viewed Mase as equal to Trigga, but then suddenly things began to change. All of a sudden she'd started only asking to speak to Trigga and he would relay the information to Mase after the meetings. Soon he was seeing Queen less and less and Trigga was sending the messages to him from her.

When Mase finally asked what the deal was, Trigga told him that Queen had told him that she'd rather only deal with him. He said that there was something about Mase that didn't sit right with her and she wanted Trigga to get rid of him. Being the loyal person Trigga was, he refused to leave his brother out and told her that it was either both of them or none of them. Queen agreed because of her admiration of Trigga, but she still refused to meet with Mase.

That was the last straw for Mase. He had to get rid of Trigga because he could see that with Trigga alive, he would forever live in his shadow. He would never be able to be happy as long as his brother had something to do with it. But Trigga wasn't the only one that had to be handled, so did that bitch Queen for choosing Trigga over him. He would take her money, which was more than enough to survive off of. After that he was going to get rid of her the same way he did his own mother, one shot straight to the dome.

"Where you at, nigga?" Mase asked once Trigga answered his phone.

"I'm here back in the A. Yo' ass must be on E," Trigga laughed and Mase gritted his teeth. Just like Trigga to laugh at the thought of Mase needing him.

"Yeah, man. I heard Lloyd bout to be out. You ready to finish this job?" Mase quizzed him.

"Fa' sho, my nigga."

"Can I borrow somethin' before we get started tho'?" Mase asked .

"Yeah, I'm busy right now. but I'll call you and we can meet up tonight so you can get the stacks, a'ight? Peace, my nigga."

"Peace."

Mase hung up the phone and then grabbed his .9 mm off the counter of the bathroom of the roach motel he was staying in. Whether Lloyd was out or not, Mase was ready to go ahead and get this shit over with tonight. He'd just figure out the other details regarding Queen later.

NINETEEN

"Damn, Keesh, what's goin' on? You look like you just seen a damn ghost," Tish said as she stared into Keisha's face.

Keisha stared at Tish with a quizzical and vacant expression on her face. She was looking at her, but her mind was on what she thought she'd just seen.

That couldn't have been Trigga outside of my window. It's not possible…am I seeing shit again? She thought to herself.

"Helllllllooooooo?" Tish asked as she waved her hand in front of Keisha's face and tried to bring her attention back into the room.

"Okay, you might think I'm buggin' but I'm not," Keisha said slowly as she rolled her eyes to the ceiling and replayed what she'd seen in her mind. She swallowed and then opened her mouth to continue. "Bitch…I could've sworn I saw Trigga's ass outside."

Tish gave her a blank look and waited for her to tell her it was a joke, but when Keisha didn't laugh or take back her comments, Tish's mouth dropped open.

"You lyin'! So what you sayin', we just talked his ass up or something?"

"I'm sayin' that I could've sworn I saw him out there. He wasn't in his car though. He was in a Porsche, I think," Keisha said as she tried to recall what kind of vehicle it was that she had seen.

"Helllll yeah, that's that nigga. Nobody rolling up in this dump ridin' in no damn Porsche," Tish joked. She stopped laughing when she saw that Keisha hadn't cracked a smile.

"Listen, Keesh…only way to know is to call him and ask if that was him. No need sitting there looking crazy about it. Just ask him."

Keisha nodded her head and lay back on the bed with her phone in her hand. Noticing that Tish still had her eyes focused directly on her face , Keisha moved her head up and looked at Tish.

"Well, damn, can I get some privacy?" she asked her with her hands in the air.

Sighing loudly and taking the extra mile to appear annoyed, Tish rolled her eyes and rolled off the bed.

"Fine. I was just tryin' to be supportive, but wait and see if I ever help your ass again."

"Yeah, yeah, yeah…I love you too Tee," Keisha yelled out as Tish walked out of the room and slammed the door behind her.

Keisha rolled her own eyes and shook her head at Tish's fake attitude before pulling her attention back to the phone in her hand. She scrolled to Trigga's number and then paused before hitting the call button. They hadn't spoken to each other since he'd left. All communication had been through text and it was always text that *he* initiated. Mustering up all of the courage she possibly could, Keisha hit the call button and waited.

She held her breath as the phone rang and rang…and rang some more.

Damn, Keisha thought to herself. She was hoping that this wouldn't happen because then she would have more decisions to make about whether she should leave a message, or call back…follow up with a text, or what? Then just as she was about to hang up the phone, he answered.

"Hello?"

Trigga's voice seeped through the phone, into her ear and danced around her eardrum. The deep, calm and authoritative tone that he spoke with was enough to melt away her panties in an instant. She felt the butterflies in her stomach return. They were the same butterflies she had whenever she saw his name flash across her screen and she knew that he was texting her. Her heartbeat sped up and all of a sudden she felt hot. She opened her mouth to speak, but no words came out.

"Keisha?" he asked. The way her name rolled off of his tongue only made her situation worse. Now she felt the butterflies between her legs as her sex started to respond to his voice as if it was trained to react to his command…Was that normal?

"Trigga, I—I thought I…Are you in town?" she blurted out, then slapped her forehead with her hand and groaned inwardly. She'd wanted to speak with a little more ease and casually go into her reason for calling him, but in her nervousness, her brain had died and her mouth went straight to the point.

"In town?" he asked her slowly. Keisha thought she could hear the evidence of a smile in his voice, but she was so mortified at her inability to have a normal adult conversation that she didn't think on it.

"Yeah…I thought—well, I know this is gonna sound crazy, but I could've sworn that I saw you at…you know what?" Keisha fell into nervous laughter as Trigga sat silently on the other end. "Just forget it. I'm buggin'."

"Naw, ma, you ain't buggin'. I was there," he said finally. Keisha stopped laughing abruptly and her eyes widened at his admission.

"You were in front of my apartment? I *knew* I saw you! Why didn't you call me, or knock on the door, or— " Keisha shut her mouth suddenly, afraid that she was babbling or probably sounded like one of the thirsty chicks that Trigga was used to dealing with.

"I wanted to…I thought about it, but I—something came up," he said.

"Ohhhh…Okay," Keisha said unable to hide the disappointment in her voice.

"I'll talk to you later, a'ight?"

"A'ight," Keisha responded. She pulled the phone away from her ear and was about to hang up, but then changed her mind.

Fuck it, she thought to herself. She looked down at the phone and realized that Trigga still hadn't hung up either.

"Trigga, you there?" she asked as she pulled it back to her ear.

There was silence for a few beats, but then his mellow voice came through and made her toes curl.

"Yeah…"

Keisha bit her bottom lip, closed her eyes and blurted out her next sentence quickly before she lost her courage.

"Do you wanna—can you come over for dinner later on? I can cook and I'm good at it. I know it may have been a while since you've had a home cooked meal and—"

"No," he said cutting her off.

Keisha's face fell and her heart dropped to the floor. She felt like someone had reached inside her, grabbed hold of her insides, twisted them and then ripped them out of her body. Trigga's words were like a slap in the face. The butterflies were gone and emptiness replaced them. She felt tears sting her eyes and her cheeks flushed red with shame.

Swallowing hard, Keisha cleared her throat so she could at least say goodbye before hanging up the phone and vowing to never call him back. But when she opened up her mouth, nothing came out, so she just shook her head, pressed the button to end the call and then fell back on her bed, trying to will herself not to cry.

Maybe I was wrong about him, she thought to herself. She'd thought they had a connection. Although he'd never really said anything to make her believe it, she still had the feeling that he was feeling her for some reason.

Seconds later her phone rang. Keisha grabbed it with the intention of ignoring the call. She wasn't in the mood to talk to anyone, but then she noticed the name on the screen. Just seeing the letters spelling his name did things to her even though she'd been about to crawl into a hole and die seconds before. After debating for a second on whether she should answer the call or not, she answered, but didn't say anything.

"The fuck you hung up on me for?" Trigga's blurted out as soon as she answered.

"Because you said—"

"I know what I said," he responded matter-of-factly.

Confused, Keisha frowned up her face as she held the phone in her hand, "But—"

"I'm not gonna let your ass be in the kitchen all day tryin' to cook for a nigga on our first date," Trigga said. "I'll cook for you instead. Be ready 'round six and I'll pick you up."

A smile broke out on Keisha's face and once again she was back to the giddy schoolgirl state she'd been in when she'd first heard his voice. It was incredible how one sentence—even one word from Trigga totally changed her whole vibe.

"Okay, that's cool, but...can you cook?" Keisha asked.

"I look like a cookin' ass nigga?"

Keisha rolled her eyes. "Not really...but what you tryin' to say about cookin' ass niggas?"

Trigga held in a laugh as he thought about the first night they'd met.

"Hell naw, I can't cook for shit," he responded. Keisha was totally caught off guard and didn't know how to respond until she heard Trigga's deep sexy ass laugh come through the phone. It put her at ease immediately.

"So if a nigga cooking for you then you know you must be important," he added.

"Well, if I eat it then you must know you're important," Keisha responded laughing on her own.

"That's what up," Trigga said. "I'll hit you up when I'm on my way."

"Okay," Keisha said and then hung up the phone.

As soon as she dropped her iPhone on the bed, Tish barged into the room with a big ass grin on her face.

"OH MY GOD, when he said 'no', I almost had a heart attack out there! Bitch, I thought your ass had been straight played for a fool. I was about to go pull out the liquor and chick flicks, so I could help you brush that shit off!" Tish said as she jumped on the bed.

"TISH! I know your ass wasn't eavesdropping. And what kind of device your Inspector Gadget ass used to hear Trigga through the phone?" Keisha asked her as she sat up and gawked at her friend.

"Girl, who in the world couldn't hear that sexy ass voice?" she asked playfully. Keisha fell out laughing. "Naw, but on some real shit, your volume loud as hell. But anyways, get your ass up so we can figure out what you gonna wear!"

TWENTY

"How my favorite ladies doin'?" Kenyon asked as he walked into the mother room that he'd had made just for Dior and Karisma.

Karisma was only a few weeks old, but she was the smartest and most beautiful thing that Kenyon had ever seen. She was cute as a button and looked just like her mother as if Dior had made her on her own. Dior was happy about that. She'd never tell a soul, but the last thing she wanted to do was have to stare at a mini-Lloyd all day. After what he'd done to her, she'd been traumatized for days. The only thing that saved her was the birth of her beautiful daughter a week later.

Kenyon had been the perfect father for Karisma from day one as if he really was her biological father. Dior had a complicated pregnancy that resulted in a C-section so when she first came home, she wasn't able to care for her daughter like she wanted to. Kenyon stepped right in and did everything so she didn't have to lift a finger. Plus, he cared for her , and tended to her every beck and call. He was superman.

Seeing Kenyon with Karisma was the most beautiful thing on Earth to her. Having lost her own biological father at a young age, Dior had been raised by a stepfather who had adored her the same way that Kenyon seemed to love Karisma. Looking at their interaction made her miss her own stepfather, who she hadn't spoken to since she married Lloyd.

Maybe he will be open to a truce now that he has a granddaughter, Dior thought as she looked down in Karisma's eyes.

The funny thing about the little girl was that she had the same light brown eyes and long eyelashes that Kenyon had, although there was no possible way that he was her father. Dior and Kenyon hadn't started having sex until after she was already pregnant. Kenyon and Lloyd were cousins who shared the same genes so it made sense that one's child may have similar features to the other.

"We're great. I think Princess Kay may be ready for a nap. As soon as she goes down, I'm going to lay down also," Dior said. As if on cue, Karisma yawned and closed her eyes. Dior's heart leaped for joy. She loved holding her daughter, but she was tired. Breast-feeding every two hours was crazier than she'd even imagined it would be.

"A'ight," Kenyon said with a smile as he looked both of them over to make sure they were okay. "I have to run an errand and I'll be right back. Shouldn't take too long. You need anything?"

"Nope, I'm fine!" Dior said with a smile, but Kenyon focused in on her bloodshot eyes.

"Rest up, baby," he said giving her a kiss on the forehead. "I'll be back before you wake up."

Dior nodded her head and saw that Karisma had fallen into a peaceful sleep just that quickly. Her thin lips were parted and her almond-shaped eyes were closed. Kenyon took one final look at the both of them. His heart was at peace and it would stay that way as soon as he did what he needed to do.

"Mr. St. Michaels, how are you today?" West asked as he walked into the small interrogation room at the Fulton County Police Department in downtown Atlanta.

He was in the best mood he'd been in probably since before he started his job in Atlanta. That morning he woke up with a frown on his face as he cursed life for dealing him the hand that he was holding, but then everything changed after he got the phone call he'd been praying for. Maybe there was a God. Maybe that God did love him.

"Hello, Detective West," Kenyon said as he eyed West suspiciously. He looked obviously uncomfortable about being there, but it didn't matter to West at all. As long as Kenyon did what he needed him to do, he could be as snappy as he wanted to be.

"Well, so we both know why you're here so I'm going to skip the preliminaries. What can you give me on James Lloyd Evans, also known as Black?" West questioned after he pushed the button on the recorder in between them.

Kenyon eyed it suspiciously and twisted up his nose in disgust.

"I'm being recorded?"

"Standard procedure," West said with a smile.

"Well, I ain't sayin' shit until you can guarantee that my name won't be on shit. I got a family now and I need to protect them. That's the only reason I'm up in this shit to begin with. I need to protect mine," Kenyon said as he glared at West.

West groaned inwardly. He didn't care about all this 'man of the year' shit that Kenyon was spitting and he cared even less about sticking his neck out to spare the life of a low-down street thug. He and his family were everything that was wrong about this nation to him. They were the scum of the Earth.

But in order to bring them all down, he had to play the game.

"I promise to do everything in my power to protect your family," West said. When Kenyon didn't respond, he continued. "And your name won't be on shit."

That did it. Kenyon relaxed somewhat and laid back in his seat. Pulling out a blunt from his pocket, he twisted it around in his fingers for a bit as he looked at it, then he held it out to West.

"You got a light?" he asked him.

West fought the urge to turn up his nose and slap Kenyon's hand out of his face. Instead, he gritted his teeth and reached down in his pocket.

"Here you go," West said as he held out the lighter to Kenyon, but he didn't move. Finally catching his drift, West sighed, lit the lighter and then held the fire to Kenyon's blunt. Kenyon took two quick pulls and then sat back with the lit blunt in between his fingers.

West watched him with disgust and waited until Kenyon had smoked nearly half of the blunt. Just as West was about to lose his patience and kick Kenyon out of the building, he spoke.

"Okay, Detective West," Kenyon said. "What is that you want to know?"

A sinister smile grew on West's face and he leaned forward.

"You can start at the beginning. We got all day. I'm on your time."

TWENTY-ONE

Keisha frowned as she looked at herself in the mirror. She was beginning to think that leaving Tish in charge of her look for the night might have been a mistake. Here she was standing in six-inch heels, a short bandage dress and a full face of make-up for something that she had the feeling was supposed to be a casual dinner date. But, according to Tish, Trigga had only seen Keisha at her absolute worst the last couple times since they first met at the club, so she had to show him on their first date what she looked like at her best.

Keisha had to admit one thing though, Tish did the damn thing. She did her make-up, curled her hair to perfection and even did her nubby nails. Keisha was on point for a date with an A-list celebrity, so there wasn't a doubt in her mind that Trigga would at least be impressed even if she was severely overdressed.

"You ready? He just texted and said he's on his way," Tish said handing Keisha her iPhone.

"Damn, you checkin' my phone now?" Keisha asked as she snatched it from her fingers.

"Mmhmm, and responding too. I told him that you'll be waiting," Tish smiled and Keisha rolled her eyes at her.

"You sure this isn't way too much? I mean, I'm just going to his hotel room," Keisha asked as she looked back in the mirror and started fussing with her hair.

Tish twisted up her lips as she squinted at Keisha's image in the mirror.

"You're right, there is one thing that you need to do," Tish told her.

"What?"

"Take off your panties if you have some on. I forgot you were goin' back to the room so you need to be prepared to give his sexy ass the goods!"

"Bitch! You are so crazy," Keisha laughed. It was just what she needed to take the edge off.

"No, I'm tellin' your ass what's real. At least make sure you don't have no granny panties on."

"Um, I don't own no damn granny panties!"

"You sure?" Tish asked crinkling her brows. "Because those Marilyn Monroe draws you bought the other day—"

Keisha sucked her teeth and pushed past Tish just as her phone started to chime. She looked down and saw a text from Trigga.

Here was all it said.

"Damn, that was quick! That nigga was burning up rubber to see your ass!" Tish laughed as Keisha walked towards the front door.

She grabbed her purse off the counter in the kitchen and checked to make sure that she had breath-mints. Pausing at the door, she took a deep breath and tried to relax.

As she grabbed the doorknob, she looked back and Tish gave her the thumbs-up sign. Keisha shot her a nervous smile and then opened the door.

As soon as she stepped out she almost ran smack-dab into a bouquet of roses.

"Oh my God!" she gasped as she covered her mouth in shock.

"You want me to put these inside?" Trigga asked peeking over the bouquet that had been covering his face. Keisha looked from him to the roses and nodded her head silently.

Noticing that he looked a little uneasy, she moved to the side and allowed him to walk inside. Trigga walked in, his strong manly scent mixed with his cologne trailing behind him. Keisha took a deep breath of it as he passed. It was like an elixir that ignited every part of her body. Every nerve ending shot off and yearned for him.

As he bent over slightly and placed the vase on the table, Tish walked out from the back with her hand out-stretched and a big ass grin on her face.

"Hi! I'm Tish," she greeted him.

Trigga paused for a minute and then shot her a grin back. Keisha caught feelings for a second when she saw Tish nearly swoon when he smiled at her. Trigga accepted her hand and shook it.

"Nice to meet you, Tish. I'm Trigga."

"Oh, I know. Keisha talks about you *alllll* the time," Tish blabbed. Keisha was mortified. She could feel the sting of embarrassment as all of the blood in her body traveled to her face, making her cheeks flush red.

"TISH!" Keisha gasped.

Trigga and Tish both turned to look at her and Keisha tried, with difficulty, to relax.

"I mean, damn…ain't nothing sacred anymore?" Keisha said as she looked at Tish. She laughed nervously to lighten the mood in the room.

"My bad," Tish said. "She actually don't really talk about you all that much."

"TISH!" Keisha yelled out again and Trigga chuckled.

"It's okay," he said. "I mean…I burned rubber to get here, right?" he asked laughing. It was his attempt at a joke to lighten the mood and ease Keisha's embarrassment, but it only made it worse as she realized that he'd heard them talking about him while he stood at the door.

"Oh, God, let's just go," Keisha groaned. Trigga walked to her, flashed her a smile and then grabbed her hand.

"Yep, let's go, because I don't want the oatmeal I made you to get cold."

Keisha did a double-take at him with wide eyes.

"What?" he asked feigning confusion. "You don't like oatmeal? What southern chick don't like oatmeal? I got sweet tea, too!"

After watching her struggle to find the right words to say in response, Trigga started laughing and Keisha relaxed.

"C'mon, Keesh. You know I ain't cook you no damn oatmeal," he said.

Keisha tightened her grip on his hand as he led her out to his car, an all black Porsche truck.

"I mean…I'm more of a PB & J sandwich man, anyways. You ever used Goobers for a PB & J? That shit be bumpin' like a muthafucka," he said with a grin.

Keisha laughed as he helped her in the car. She was totally and thoroughly caught up by this man and she wasn't even entirely sure why.

About an hour later Keisha was so full that she felt like she would burst wide open. Trigga had either told her the world's biggest lie, or he'd found a way to have the hotel staff come in and prepare dinner for them and make it look like a home-cooked meal. Saying that he was a bad cook was definitely a set up. He was the exact opposite.

For dinner, Trigga had prepared a small piece of 'southern flava' as he called it. He said he'd never asked her what her favorite food was, but because she looked like a traditional southern beauty, he decided to cook a small portion of all of the typical southern food he could think of in hopes that he hit some of her favorites. When Keisha walked in, she was greeted by a table full of baked mac and cheese, green beans, black-eyed peas, oven fried chicken, cracklin' cornbread, yams, yellow rice, parmesan-encrusted meatloaf, baked pork chops, broccoli casserole…he had everything she could think of. And that wasn't even counting the desserts. She had her choice of peach cobbler, apple pie, red velvet cake…it was amazing.

"How in the world did you have time to do this?" Keisha asked him as she looked at him.

Trigga was dressed simply in dark jeans, dress shoes and a black dress shirt with his Cuban link gold chain hanging around his neck. He had the sleeves rolled up to his muscular biceps as he cleaned up the table. As he grabbed her plate from the table he shrugged.

"I just got started after we got off the phone. Didn't take all that long actually. I told the hotel staff what I was doing and they let me use their kitchen."

"And they didn't help you at all?" Keisha asked narrowing her eyes with suspicion. Trigga caught her drift and looked at her with a smile breaking out on his face.

"Naw, I cooked it. They just helped by stayin' out my way."

"Well, how you learn to cook like this?" Keisha asked him as she rubbed her stomach and looked at the remaining dishes on the table. She wondered if it would be rude to ask for a to-go plate. The food had been scrumptious.

"My mother, God rest her soul, she used to make me come in the kitchen with her and cook. She taught a nigga that if you don't cook you don't eat."

As Trigga spoke about his mother, Keisha saw a hint of sadness enter his eyes. Then he shook it off and kept removing the plates from the table and placed them in the kitchen.

"I mean pretty chicks like you don't be cooking no more." He flashed Keisha a smile. "Yo' ass fine and all but you look like a nigga would be eating bologna sandwiches fuckin' wit' you."

"I can cook!" Keisha said as she crossed her arms in front of her chest and faked an attitude.

Trigga laughed and grabbed the last of the plates and took them to the kitchen. After they were all gone, he grabbed Keisha by her arm and brought her to her feet. Before saying anything, he just sat and stared deeply into her eyes. It seemed like he wanted to say something, but he didn't.

Keisha could feel her knees grow weak as she stared at him. Her eyes dropped to his lips. They were perfect; just thick enough to be considered juicy. He had suckable lips.

Trigga was fighting an inner battle. Keisha was fuckin' up his head and she didn't even know it. He was supposed to be spending the night plotting how he was going to get his job done and get back to New York City. Instead, he had spent all day playing Mr. Betty Crocker. Keisha had a nigga in the kitchen baking and whipping up meals like he was sweet, or some shit. Instead of putting bullets in a nigga's skull, he was pulling out measuring cups and shit. What part of the fuckin' game was that?

Turning to her, he grabbed her around her waist and pulled her into his arms. There was something about her that felt so familiar to him, but he couldn't place it. Either way, he felt drawn to her from day one and here it was, over a month since they first met and he still had that feeling. It was like he felt like he would be missing out on something if he didn't keep her around. Chicks like this could fuck a nigga's head up and he knew it, but maybe he was ready to get a little fucked up.

And a nigga was ready to get fucked. Truth was, he hadn't had any pussy for over a month and his dick was hard as hell. He wondered what Keisha would do if he tried her.

*Shit…this the first date, but hell, she done known my ass for over a month. We saved each other's lives…*he thought in his head.

He didn't want her to feel disrespected if he tried something on the first date, but he was feeling her. What he felt was beyond just wanting sex, but a nigga would be lying if he said he didn't want sex. Plus, that whole 'having sex on the first date makes you a hoe' shit was played out. No, fuckin' a *gang* of niggas on the first night made you a hoe. Trigga could tell from looking at Keisha that she wasn't that type of chick.

As soon as he was about to bend his head to suck on her pretty ass neck, his phone rang and he groaned inwardly. Although she tried to play it off, he saw Keisha sigh in disappointment as well. He tried to hold down the smirk that eased up on his face.

Ahhh, so you wanted it too, I see, he thought. There was the green light he had needed.

"Let me get rid of this right quick," Trigga said pulling out his phone.

"It's cool. I gotta go to the bathroom," Keisha said and walked away.

"Down the hall and to the left," he called behind her.

Mase, he thought as he looked at his phone. He'd totally forgotten that he had told him earlier to stop by and grab some money until they got paid for Queen's job.

"Aye, nigga, you here?" Trigga said as he answered the phone.

"Yeah, I'm boutta come up," Mase responded.

"Naw, don't do that! I got company!"

"Nigga, I'm already on the fuckin' elevator. You in the penthouse right? Just tell me the code so this shit will go up. I'm stuck on the third floor."

Trigga sighed and ran his hand over his face. Then he looked down the hall. Keisha was still in the bathroom.

"It's Mom's birthday. 03-29," Trigga responded. The line went silent. "You there?"

"Yeah, see you," Mase said.

Keisha looked at herself in the mirror and willed herself to calm down. She was in a sexual frenzy and she was trying to keep herself from getting caught up.

"Bitch, you cannot have sex with that nigga, so get it out of your mind!" she told herself. But the reality was her body was telling her one thing, although she knew that she should have been doing another.

There were two very good reasons that she couldn't have sex with Trigga tonight. One was because she didn't want him to think of her as a hoe. She'd had sex with Lloyd on the first night and it was probably why he didn't respect her once they started their relationship. He saw her as a hoe and eventually he ended up treating her as one.

The second reason was because she still hadn't bothered to get her tattoo of Lloyd's name on her ass covered up. The last thing she wanted Trigga to see was her tattoo because then she would have a lot of explaining to do. He didn't even know that she knew Lloyd prior to that night at the club and she wanted to keep it that way. If he ever found out, she knew he would think that she was a part of the ambush that had almost killed him. He might put a bullet straight through her right smack in the middle of an orgasm if he saw that tattoo during sex. A cute stranger asks for you to take her home and the next thing you know you're being thrown into an ambush set up by her ex-boyfriend? There would be no way to explain that level of coincidence to him.

No, I can't have sex with this man, she told herself again and nodded at her reflection in the mirror. She had to play it cool until she got everything together. She heard voices coming from the front room. There were two voices.

Is someone out there? she thought, but then shook it off as she got herself ready to stop hiding out in the bathroom, giving herself the celibacy speech.

Running her hand over her dress, she took a deep breath and opened the bathroom door. As soon as she raised her eyes from the tile floor, she focused in on a figure at the end of the hall who was standing in front of the entrance of the elevator that served as the entryway into the penthouse. Her heart dropped and panic took hold of her body. Her legs began shaking at the knees as her feet melded with the ground as if they had anchors tied to them. She couldn't move. She was paralyzed by her fear.

"Damn, nigga, you cooked and shit," Mase said as Keisha watched him from the side. She felt the urge to pee and although she felt the liquid begin to seep out from her as the sensation grew stronger, she couldn't move or stop it.

Suddenly she saw Mase move to turn towards where she was standing and her 'flight or flee' instinct kicked in. Within a second, Keisha ducked into the room adjacent to her and pushed the door quietly closed behind her. Her breathing came out in sharp gulps as she leaned against the door and cried silently. Her hands were trembling and her legs were as well—almost to the point that she could barely stand on her own. Sliding down the wall beside her, she fell down on the floor, pulled her legs to her chest, rested her head on her knees and sobbed.

Lloyd was right. At the hospital he had told her that Trigga was working with Mase. They all were trying to kill her and this was the end.

Tonight she would die.

TWENTY-TWO

"Listen, man, you gone have to move your ass up out of here. I got a date," Trigga said growing increasingly impatient.

"Damn, nigga, well what she look like? She got a sister?" Mase asked staring down the hall. "She still in the damn bathroom? What she doin'? Shittin' or something?"

Trigga frowned and clenched his teeth as he looked at his brother.

"Mase, I ain't gone tell yo' ass no more. Shuffle yo' muthafuckin' feet."

Mase turned to Trigga and gave him a hard look. His hand grazed his waist and he felt the steel that was tucked down in the waistband of his pants. Biting his lip, he told himself that this was his moment. The moment he could end it all and stop living in his brother's shadow. He had a few bands in his pants now and that was enough to hold him over until he figured out how he was gonna get at Queen and help himself to her wealth. All he had to do now was put a bullet through this nigga's head in front of him.

"You hard of hearin'?" Trigga asked him with a snarl. He took a quick look down the hall. He didn't know what was holding Keisha up, but he hoped she wasn't aware of how he was going back and forth with his brother.

"Naw," Mase said cooly. "I get it."

Mase reached down to his waist and put his hand on the handle of the weapon as he stared into Trigga's grey eyes.

I could do it now, he thought. *I could end it all. This nigga won't be around to make me look like I ain't shit any longer. He can take his spot in hell next to mama and then Queen can join him.*

"By the way, while I was home I spoke to Queen about you," Trigga said.

At the sound of Queen's name, Mase's hand dropped to his side and he narrowed his eyes at Trigga with curiosity.

"What about?"

"I told her that I wouldn't be doin' nothin' else with her unless you're in it. We have a conference call scheduled tomorrow to talk to her about future jobs." Trigga glanced down the hall to make sure that Keisha wasn't listening and he said in a hushed voice, "She got some more niggas we need to handle for her after this job. She already sent us a nice lump sum of money for the job I got stashed for us."

Shit! Mase thought to himself. He couldn't put a bullet in Trigga right now. Queen would grow suspicious if he missed the call, plus he needed money. The price of pussy was high in Atlanta.

"A'ight," Mase said nodding his head. "I'll be over here tomorrow for the call and my share of the money"

Turning around, Mase walked over to the elevator and pushed the button. The doors opened and he walked on. As the doors closed, he cursed himself for missing another opportunity to settle the score, but made a promise that he would follow through after the conference call with Queen the next day. The information he'd get after the call might prove to be useful.

Trigga walked down the hall and frowned when he noticed the bathroom light was off and the door was opened, but no one was inside.

"Keisha?" he called out, but no one answered.

The hell did she go? he thought.

Walking back down the hall, he grabbed the doorknob and opened the door. As soon as it opened, a glass vase went sailing through the air directly at his head.

"THE FUCK?!" Trigga yelled as he ducked and turned on the lights.

As soon as the light came on, his eyes focused on Keisha who was standing against the wall with an expression of terror scrawled across her face.

"Get away from me!" she screeched as she cried.

"Keisha! What the hell is wrong with you?" Trigga yelled out. He started moving forward into the room, but then stopped when he saw her fall to the carpeted floor and cower beneath him as she cried.

"Get away from me! Please!" she yelled out.

And the like a case of déjà vu it came to him. Trigga suddenly remembered where he knew her from. She was the junkie he had helped when he was staking out Lloyd's place nearly three months ago and trying to devise a plan on how to best get at him. She was the woman who had fought him from underneath a black Cadillac SUV as he tried to help her. She was a junkie. He'd fallen for a crack head.

Just like that a switch clicked in Trigga's brain and he put a wall up. He couldn't allow himself to fall for this woman. He had enough shit circling in his world. Too much was going on for him to play savior to a woman who obviously had wasted the one chance he'd given her to get her life together.

"Keisha, you're high...I'm not going to hurt you," Trigga said calmly. "Get up. I'll take you home."

"I'm not fuckin' high! You and that nigga, Mase, are trying to kill me! Lloyd told me! I knew it! I knew I shouldn't have trusted you!" she screamed out.

That got Trigga's attention. Narrowing his eyes, he searched her face as she continued to cry.

"How do you know Mase?" Trigga asked her.

"What do you mean?" Keisha asked as she stared at him. "He tried to kill me! He was there...that night we got ambushed, he was the one who shot me! He came to the hospital when I woke up and he tried to kill me!"

"You got to be mistaken, Keisha," Trigga said slowly still thinking she was high on something. "Mase is my twin brother. He wasn't part of the ambush…that would mean he tried to kill me too."

The tears left Keisha's face and she stood up slowly. Though the tears were gone, her eyes still glistened. Her face was straight and as Trigga looked in her eyes, he could tell that she was lucid. Her pupils weren't dilated. She wasn't high at all.

"Mase is working with Lloyd. That day I found you in the grass in front of Lloyd's condo, Lloyd wasn't in there. Mase was. They were trying to kill me and Mase was going to chop up my body into pieces. The only reason I escaped was because he tried to force me to give him head and I bit his penis til' he bled." Keisha shivered as she replayed that day in her mind. "He had black marks on his penis. Like burn marks. He's in on it. He tried to kill me. I'm not lying."

Trigga was looking at Keisha, but he had long ago zoned out and was in his own thoughts.

How did she know about the black marks on Mase's penis?

When they were younger, some boys had found out about the black burn marks on Mase's penis during gym and started teasing him about it. Trigga ended up fighting them for picking on his brother, but instead of Mase being grateful, it only seemed to make him angry. Trigga wondered to himself where the marks came from, but every time he tried to ask Mase he became angry, so Trigga finally dropped the topic.

Keisha watched Trigga intently as he thought, hoping that he would believe her. Suddenly, he turned on his heels and took off running.

As Trigga entered the front room, he banged his finger against the button on the elevator until the doors opened. He jumped in, hit the button for the doors to close and then mashed the button for the lobby. He had to catch Mase before he left. Someone was lying and someone was telling the truth, but he would find out who was who tonight.

When he got to the lobby, he ran out of the double doors and right into the street just as Mase's whip turned the corner. He was too late.

Trigga stood in the night air right in the middle of the street and tried to make sense of the last few minutes of his life. Could Keisha be right? Could his brother be trying to kill him? Or was it Keisha who couldn't be trusted?

One thing for sure, Trigga thought as he walked back into the lobby of the hotel, *someone is bullshittin' but Mase will be back to talk to Queen tomorrow and I'll find out every fuckin' thing then.*

Note From THE AUTHORS!

WE APPRECIATE YOU! Thank you for taking out the time to read this novel. It was written from the heart and we hope you enjoyed it. Make sure to leave a review! We read them. We love them.

Peace, love & blessings to everyone. We love allllll of you!

&

LEO SULLIVAN

CPSIA information can be obtained
at www.ICGtesting.com
Printed in the USA
LVOW04s1323180316

479771LV00022B/428/P